GREED CAN BE DEADLY

SAGE GARDENS COZY MYSTERY

CINDY BELL

CHAPTER 1

"*B*e still, Eddy!" Samantha rolled her eyes, then smoothed down Eddy's tie. Each time she tried to get the knot even, he would shift from one foot to the other, or drop his shoulders.

"I'm going to be late if you keep fiddling with that thing." Eddy frowned as he looked into her eyes.

"Do you want it tied right or not?" Samantha raised an eyebrow as she gazed back at him. She had to hide a smile. Even though they exchanged words in cross tones, they were playing a familiar game. Eddy had to be tough, and she had to remind him that he wasn't as tough as he thought.

"Yes, I do. I'm sorry, I'm just a bit nervous." He

took a deep breath and held it so that he wouldn't move again.

"Nervous about what? I thought this guy was an old friend of yours?" She finished knotting his tie and smoothed it down one last time. "There, dapper as always."

"Dapper." Eddy rolled his eyes. "That's a bit of an exaggeration."

"Why are you nervous?" She stared straight into his dark blue eyes. It was unusual for her to see so much concern in them. "He's your friend."

"He was my partner, for the last few years that I worked. He was just a young pup when he got paired with me. He had just been promoted to detective. In some ways, he was like a son to me." He lifted one shoulder in a mild shrug. "I'm just surprised that he wanted to get together. It's been a while, and honestly, I thought I bonded with him more than he bonded with me."

"I'm not surprised at all. I've seen the way the other officers look up to you. Even Detective Brunner admires your experience." Samantha smiled as she smoothed down the collar of his suit jacket. "I hope you have a wonderful time."

"I'm going to do my best. Thanks for helping me out, Sam." He reached up to touch the top of his head. He fumbled over his thinning, brown hair, then scowled. "Now, where did I put my hat?"

"You should go without it. You look good as is." Samantha turned to pick up her purse. "I can't wait to hear all about it in the morning."

"Is Walt still up for breakfast?" He grabbed his hat from the back of his couch and set it on the top of his head.

"Yes, and Jo said she'll be there, too. About eight. Unless you're too wiped out from tonight to join us." She glanced over her shoulder at him with a wide smile. "I know what it can be like to get together with old friends."

"Oh sure, I'll be crawling back here at three in the morning. What do you think I am, twenty?" Eddy shook his head as he walked her to the door.

"You might as well be." Samantha patted his cheek. "You're grinning like a kid."

"Yeah, yeah, yeah. Have a good night, Sam." He grabbed his trench coat off the rack beside the door. Although, the days were warm the nights were still quite chilly, and it had been raining quite a bit recently. As Eddy pulled on his coat, he felt a buzz of excitement course through his veins. Ever since he retired from the police force there had been a subtle gnawing in the pit of his stomach, as if he'd forgotten something important. He lived and breathed crime before he retired, and now that he lived in Sage Gardens, a retirement community, his life was a lot calmer. At times he wasn't sure how he would survive it.

After Samantha left, Eddy grabbed his keys and headed out the door. When Colin contacted him, he was surprised to say the least. It had been over a year since the last time he spoke with him, and that was only a brief call about a case they had once worked together. Out of the blue he'd reached out to Eddy, and asked to meet for drinks.

This was unusual, and left Eddy very curious about what his friend wanted to discuss. On his way to the bar he thought about the last case they were involved in. He was just about to retire, as the rules dictated it, and this was the case that made him realize that it was the right time. Colin had drawn his weapon in response to a suspect spinning around to face them and pulling his weapon. But Eddy had struggled to get his weapon out of its holster. He knew that he was losing his edge. If it hadn't been for Colin's quick response, they could have both been killed. Colin never said a word about it, he didn't have to.

Eddy parked outside the bar and took a moment

to adjust his tie. Samantha had worked so hard to make it look just right, but it was a little too tight. He loosened the knot, then stepped out of the car and headed inside. It was just after dark and there were a few people scattered outside the bar. The pavement was wet from rain earlier in the day, but the sky was clear of any clouds.

Inside, there were several people crowded around the bar. It took him a few minutes to spot Colin, he was at the end of the bar, surrounded by a few men. Eddy approached him, smiling.

"Colin! It's good to see you." He clapped the younger man on the shoulder. It was a bit shocking to him to see how much Colin had aged. Even though he was thirty when they began working together, Eddy always thought of him as a young kid. In the few short years since Eddy had last worked, Colin appeared to have aged decades. Even his short, dark hair was edged with sprouts of gray.

"You too, Eddy." Colin smiled at him, just wide enough to reveal the dimples that Eddy had once teased him about. "It's about time you got here." Colin tapped his watch. "What happened to the always punctual Eddy?"

"Eh, time doesn't exist once you're retired." Eddy chuckled, but the truth was he hated being late. He climbed onto the barstool beside him. It had been a while since he was in a bar. He didn't mind a few beers here and there at home or out with friends, but he rarely spent his time in a place with overpriced drinks and potentially drunk people.

"Must be nice." Colin lifted his drink to him. "I guess one day I'll find out."

"Yes, you will." Eddy grinned. "A long, long time from now."

Eddy ordered a beer, and the two chatted a bit about life. He wasn't surprised to discover that Colin still wasn't married. The badge could often be hard on relationships.

"So, out with it, Colin." Eddy studied him closely. Maybe he didn't know him as well as he used to, but his instincts told him that he did. It seemed to him that something was on Colin's mind, something that was troubling him.

"Out with what?" He glanced up from the bottle of beer that he twirled between his palms.

"Why did you invite me here? I haven't heard from you in —"

"I know." Colin narrowed his eyes. "I'm sorry about that. My life got so busy, trying to climb the ladder, you know. But don't think I ever forgot about you, Eddy, I didn't. I got where I am because of you. You know that, right?"

"Is where you are, a good thing or a bad thing?" Eddy squinted. "Because I'm not sure if I want to take credit for that."

"Always the jokester." He sighed, then took a sip of his beer. Eddy noticed the way his jaw rippled before he spoke again. "There's something I'd like to discuss with you. But this isn't the place."

"What is it?" Eddy leaned closer to him. "If you're in some kind of trouble, you can tell me, Colin. Just because I'm retired, just because I'm not your partner anymore, that doesn't mean I can't help you."

"I know that." He locked eyes with Eddy for just a moment, then looked down at the bar. "Listen, there's a birthday party tomorrow night. It's for Hank Greer, remember him?"

"Hank, sure. He was a detective for the Shashone Precinct. Good guy, from what I remember. He had a big reputation."

"Yeah, big." He swallowed the last bit of his beer then set the bottle down rather roughly. "I think you should be there."

"Where?"

"At the birthday party. I'm going, and I'm

inviting you to go with me. You can even bring a date?" He eyed him. "What do you say?"

"Well, I barely even know the man. Not sure why you would want me to be there?" Eddy furrowed a brow, confused by the request.

"What was it you used to tell me?" A brief smile flickered across Colin's lips. "You don't have to know why, you just have to do as I say?"

Eddy smiled at the memory.

"Well, that was true then." Eddy grinned. "We were in some dodgy situations."

"It's still true, now." He stared into Eddy's eyes. "Will you be there?"

It was clear to Eddy that there was a lot more to the invitation than just a chance to spend time with an old buddy. Without thinking much more about it, he nodded.

"Of course I will, Colin." He studied his friend intently. There was a time that he could read a person's story in their eyes, but at that moment, he couldn't see anything in Colin's deep brown gaze. To him, that meant he had a lot to hide.

As he sat at the bar, Eddy couldn't help but wonder about what was going on in Colin's mind. He tried to pull more information from him about the party, but Colin avoided saying anything else about it. Instead he bought Eddy another beer, chatted about life, and shared some funny stories about mistakes he'd made on the job. It was a nice reunion, and Eddy felt as if they'd picked up right where they left off, but he couldn't shake the memory of the way Colin looked at him when he asked him to attend the party.

After they said goodnight, Eddy thought about pressing Colin for more information. He knew if he pushed him enough he would probably spill. But that wasn't the way he wanted to do things. If Colin needed him to trust him, and just follow his lead, then it was his turn to do just that. Colin had done the same during the years they had worked together. He was surprised that he didn't feel the same bond he'd had with Colin when he was younger. Perhaps too many years had passed, or they were simply two very different people now, but he viewed Colin more as a colleague than a close friend. That was for the best, he guessed, as Colin's life was full, and he doubted there would be any room in it for him.

That night as Eddy headed to bed he thought about the moments he'd spent on the job with Colin. There were some very scary experiences. The two of them always managed to stumble into danger, even if they were just investigating a minor case. More than once he'd saved Colin's life, and more than once Colin had done the same for him. As much as he wished to be back on the job, he was reassured by the fact that Colin was still there, and other officers and detectives just like him, who truly lived the job, instead of just collecting a paycheck.

Eddy fell asleep with memories of being on the job playing through his mind.

CHAPTER 2

*W*hen Eddy woke the next morning, he was confused as to why his alarm was going off. He had no reason to be up. He could sleep a bit longer if he wanted to. Then he received a text. He grabbed his phone, bleary-eyed and grumpy, and saw that it was from Samantha.

Rise and shine, we are meeting for breakfast!

"Oh, that's right." He yawned, then stretched in bed. There were times while he was working that he would go a few days with only a few hours of sleep, but since he'd retired, or perhaps since he'd passed sixty, he found that he really enjoyed sleep. In fact, sometimes he would go to bed early, just because he enjoyed it so much. He thought about canceling on breakfast, but knew that Samantha would tease him about being hungover if he did. Instead, he pulled himself out of bed and headed for the shower.

After a quick blast of hot water, he was more awake, but still not exactly eager. What he was looking forward to was the party that night. He was very curious about why Colin wanted him there. He dressed and left for the diner. As he drove to the diner he wondered what complaint Walt would have today. He was not a fan of restaurant food. Or people touching his food. Or people breathing near his food. Eddy didn't think that Walt was that wrong about not liking restaurant food. There was no way to be certain that no one had contaminated it. When he wore a badge he always wondered about that, as there were some people that didn't like serving cops. Although Walt had his quirks, Eddy would do anything he could to support him. To him, his friend was just a little finicky, and he didn't see a reason for him to have to change much. Then again, Eddy wasn't much for change himself, so maybe he needed a therapist like Walt had.

That, was never going to happen.

Eddy chuckled at the thought as he pulled into the diner. He guessed that a therapist would have a field day with his negativity, and gruff demeanor. But that therapist couldn't hope to understand his mind, when it was filled with experiences and thoughts that a doctor would never be faced with. As he approached the diner he could see through the window that Walt, Samantha, and Jo were already there. Jo had become a good friend of his, despite her history as a cat burglar. He thought he would never count a criminal as a friend, but now he did. She was reformed of course. But it still felt a little strange when he thought about the things she used to do. She had her reasons, but in his mind that didn't go far to excuse her actions. However, she'd proven herself to be a loyal, good person, that he could trust.

"Relax, I'm here." Eddy grinned as he stepped into the diner.

Samantha smiled. "It's about time!"

"I'm only a few minutes late." He sat down across from her.

"What happened to always punctual?" Walt spread a napkin across the table, then moved his plate on top of it. He then pulled out a pack of wipes and began to clean off all of his silverware.

"Things come up sometimes." Eddy shrugged,

then looked over at Samantha. "You missed me, didn't you?"

"Of course." She grinned. "So, how did drinks with your friend go?"

"Interesting." He frowned and leaned closer to her. "I don't know, something is going on, but he's not ready to tell me what it is yet."

"That sounds intriguing." Jo tapped her fingertips on the table. "What do you think it's about?"

"I'm guessing a case, something he's working on that has him nervous. He called me out of the blue, so there must be something going on. All he did was invite me to Hank Greer's birthday party, or I should say, insist that I be there."

"And you're going, right?" Jo crossed her legs as she sat back in her chair. "Because it's going to kill me if you don't find out what all of this is about."

"It's not going to kill you." Walt cut a glance in her direction. "That's a bit dramatic don't you think, Jo?"

"Someone has to be dramatic, Walt." Jo winked at him. "It might as well be me."

"She's right, though." Samantha smiled at the waitress as she approached to take their order. "It seems like a big mystery, and that always sparks all of our interest."

"I know, I know." Eddy paused as they all placed their orders. Once the waitress walked away he began to speak again. "Something is definitely up. I am not sure why he invited me to the party. Maybe he is investigating something there. Maybe it involves someone there. If it does, then it could involve some powerful people. From the way he is being so secretive it seems like he is involved in something very tricky."

"I'm not afraid of tricky." Jo smiled. "I've been in some pretty challenging situations."

"I'm sure you have." Eddy eyed her for a moment. He knew she had managed to break into buildings that had top security on them. "But people with power have the ability to ruin lives."

"That's very true." Walt frowned. "The more I learn about the financial system in this nation the more concerned I am about the few people with so much power and influence over the masses. In fact, did you know that the majority of the wealth in this country belongs to only ten people?"

"Walt." Jo put her hand on his shoulder. "We have to focus here."

"Yes, you're right." He sighed, then shook his head. "I just think that's incredibly unbalanced."

"If you think that's unbalanced you should take

into account the amount of wealth that goes undeclared by both executives and criminals." Jo raised an eyebrow.

"But the point here is we need to figure out what's going on with Colin," Samantha said.

"Hopefully, I'll find out more tonight. It may be nothing, I may be overthinking it." Eddy shrugged, then smiled at the waitress as his breakfast was delivered. "Thank you."

"Oh, this just isn't right." Walt grimaced as he looked at his plate. "There's just too much food here, it's completely out of balance for a meal. If I ate all of this it would equate to two meals, and I really like lunch, I don't want to skip lunch."

"It's okay." Jo smiled at him as she slid one of his pancakes onto her plate. "We can share."

"Thanks." Walt looked at her with a smile of relief.

"Anytime." Jo stole some of his sausage as well.

Once everyone finished their food, Walt and Jo excused themselves. They had plans to take a walk in the park as Walt insisted it was the optimal temperature for low bug interference and high Vitamin D absorption. Samantha and Eddy lingered long enough to finish their coffee. She noticed that he was uncharacteristically quiet.

"What's on your mind, Eddy?" She studied him.

"Oh, just thinking about Colin I guess. I wish we hadn't lost touch. He was such a good kid."

"He's not a kid anymore, Eddy, keep that in mind." Samantha took the last sip of her coffee. "He may need your help for other reasons."

"What do you mean?" He finished his coffee as well, then looked across the table at her.

"I mean, you're thinking he might be caught up in some kind of investigation, but what if he's the one that's in trouble? He could be involved in something that could get you into deep water." Samantha stood up from the table and dropped a few dollars on it for an extra tip.

"You think he might be caught up in something illegal?" Eddy's eyes widened as he stood up as well. "I didn't even consider that."

"All I'm saying is that people stray. Maybe he thought he could handle whatever he got himself into, and now he's discovered that he can't. I just don't want to see you pulled into something that you don't belong in." She walked beside him to the door.

"You should know me better than that, Samantha." Eddy pulled open the door for her.

"I do." Samantha stepped outside, then turned to face him as he joined her. "I know that for all of your tough exterior you have a very soft heart, and if someone you care about is in any kind of trouble, you will do whatever you can to help them. I just don't want to see you put yourself at risk."

"I'll be careful." He smiled some as he looked into her eyes. "There's something I want to ask you."

"Okay." Samantha folded her arms across her stomach and gazed back at him. "What is it?"

"I need a favor." He cleared his throat. "But only if you don't mind."

"Just spill, Eddy, you know you can talk about anything with me."

"Argue about anything, you mean." He grinned.

"At times." She nodded with a short laugh. "So, what is it?"

"I was thinking, it might help me to keep things in perspective, if I had another set of eyes there tonight. Someone with great instincts, someone that knows me well enough to pull me back if I do try to tread into something I shouldn't." Eddy tilted his head in her direction. "Someone like you?"

"You want me to go to the birthday party with you?" She quirked her brow and smiled.

"So, will you go?" His eyes narrowed.

Samantha stared back at him. She hadn't

expected that he was serious, but now she could tell that he was.

"Do you really want me to? Won't it seem a bit awkward to invite someone?" Samantha frowned as she tried to deduce whether he really wanted her to be there.

"I wouldn't have asked if I didn't want you to. Colin said I could bring someone." He shoved his hands in his pockets and glanced out at the parking lot. "If you don't want to, it's fine."

"Of course, I'll go with you, Eddy." She touched the curve of his shoulder and met his eyes when he looked back at her. "I'm just surprised that you asked, that's all."

"I'll pick you up at six?" He smiled.

"Sure, that's fine." She shivered as a strong breeze carried through the parking lot. "I thought it was supposed to warm up."

"Yes, well, those weathermen never get it right. I'll see you tonight." Eddy strode off towards his car. As she watched him go she couldn't help but wonder what he was up to. No, it wasn't unusual for him to want to spend time with her, they enjoyed each other's company immensely, when they weren't bickering over differing opinions, and often at times even when they were. But it was strange that he wanted her to come to the party with him. But now she was faced with another dilemma, what would she wear?

As Samantha drove back to her villa she thought about the options in her closet. She kept a few fancy dresses for the events that the retirement community hosted, and she had lots of casual clothes, but she didn't have much that was dressy casual. She didn't have call for it often. When she arrived at home she sorted through what she had available. She was able to piece something together, but it was hard to decide what to wear without knowing much about the party. She decided to look up the name of the man who the party would honor. There might even be some posts about it that would give her a better idea.

As she sat down at her computer her investigative mind kicked immediately into gear. She loved to dig into people, not always for the purpose of finding dirt, but just to get to know a person she otherwise might know nothing about. When she worked as an investigative journalist, her favorite part was getting to the truth. She still had a nose for it, which might account for why she wasn't more popular around Sage Gardens. Many of the women there were all about appearances, and she wasn't the type to put on an image for others. She believed that being herself was the best way to live. Not everyone understood that.

It didn't take Samantha long to find information about Hank Greer. His name was used frequently in news articles and splashed across social media. He had a dual-sided reputation. On one side, presented in news articles and headlines he was a brilliant detective, a top cop, someone that the entire community should be proud of, and celebrate. It said so, particularly on the announcement of his birthday celebration. He would be turning fifty, and the bash was also a fundraiser for charity. His large arrest record was touted, along with his involvement in youth programs. However, it only took a little more digging and reading to find the flip side of Hank Greer. There were many complaints on social media about how he bent the rules, and that he might be on the take.

Someone splashed pictures of his high-end car, large house in a rich neighborhood, and him dining at a fancy restaurant as proof that he had to be getting more funds from somewhere. There was no way to tell if the complaints were justified or not. In one the author claimed that he had been targeted by Hank, despite being innocent. The charges were later dropped as it was a case of mistaken identity. She knew that Hank could have had legitimate reasons to arrest him, but she wasn't sure.

Samantha flipped through a few more complaints and made some notes on a pad of paper. She was not the type to believe every story. She knew that police officers had a hard job and often had to make split-second decisions that no other person would ever be confronted with, and they were often criticized without people knowing the full story.

She'd written some stories about questionable actions taken by police, but had also written many about the good things they did. With all of the praise heaped on to Hank it was difficult not to weigh the good against the bad. Sure, he might have had some downfalls, but it sounded like he did quite a bit of good. Maybe it evened out in the end.

She cringed at the thought.

"You are getting old, Samantha. You know better than to think that the end justifies the means," she said to herself as she wiped her eyes which had grown dry from staring at the computer screen. At least she had an idea of whose party she would be going to that night, and why. The announcement indicated that it was at a high-end hotel, so she knew she needed to exchange her dressy casual outfit for one of the fancy dresses in the back of her closet. She smiled to herself as she smoothed the wrinkles out of the skirt. It would be nice to get to spend an evening with Eddy.

CHAPTER 3

*B*y six Samantha was ready to go, and as expected, there was a sharp knock on the door. Eddy was rarely late, and it seemed he'd decided to stick to that pattern. She slung a small purse over her shoulder and tugged the skirt of her dress down over her hips. She was rounder than she used to be in all areas of her body. The dress hugged her tight, but she was still pleased with her reflection in the mirror. When she opened the door, she found Eddy outside. She was sure he was wearing a smart suit, but she couldn't tell, as his trench coat covered everything but a few inches of pant legs and his shoes.

"Wow, Sam, you look great." He stared at her,

his mouth half-open. When he realized it, he closed his mouth and smiled.

"Just something from the back of the closet." Samantha shrugged. "I saw that the event is at Admirals Hotel, so assumed it was a dressy occasion."

"How did you find that out?" Eddy escorted her through the door of her villa, and towards his car which waited at the end of the walkway.

"I did a little research." Samantha paused as he held open the door for her. Once they were both in the car, she looked over at him. "How much do you know about Hank Greer?"

"Only that he's some kind of hometown hero. I have heard a few rumors about him being a bit rough, but never seen any proof. Everyone seems to love him. He certainly appears charming and knows how to get people on his side." He shrugged and turned the key in the ignition. "I don't know him personally, really. I only met him a couple of times years ago. Honestly, I have no idea why Colin wants me there tonight, but I'm willing to see what plays out."

"Me, too." Samantha narrowed her eyes as she decided not to reveal what she had found. It was better if Eddy came to his own conclusions. Besides, she had no idea if Hank Greer had anything to do with the problem that Colin needed help solving. She glanced over at Eddy and noticed that his usual trench coat had a large coffee stain from the cuff to almost the elbow.

"Eddy, how in the world did you spill coffee up to your elbow?" Samantha laughed as she traced the pattern with her fingertip.

"Don't ask." He rolled his eyes. "Let's just say, recliners aren't always where you expect them to be."

"Oh? Did yours get up and move?" She held back laughter.

"Yes, yes it did." He grimaced. "I'm sure I can get it cleaned."

"Maybe, or you could just buy a new coat." Samantha raised an eyebrow. "What do you think of that?"

"I think it's rubbish. My coat is just fine, it's been through a lot with me. It's not going anywhere."

"All right then." She grinned as she looked back out the window. Maybe Eddy was a little stuck in his ways, but she really enjoyed some of his quirks.

*W*hen Samantha and Eddy arrived at the hotel, the parking lot was packed.

"Wow, quite a big turn out." She stepped out of the car as Eddy held the door.

"Yes, he's a big deal, I guess." Eddy shrugged, then offered her his arm.

They were greeted at the door by a doorman, who held the door open for both of them. Eddy adjusted the collar of his trench coat and wondered if this was all a big mistake. He certainly didn't belong in a place like this. Samantha gave his arm a gentle squeeze, as if she might know what he was thinking. He smiled at her. Samantha had become a very close friend, if not a best friend. He spotted Colin in the lobby of the hotel as they stepped inside. Colin spotted him as well, and walked towards him.

"Hi, Colin, I'd like you to meet my friend, Samantha." Eddy smiled as he gestured to her.

"It's nice to meet you, Samantha." Colin smiled as he offered her his hand. "Any friend of Eddy's is a survivor." He laughed.

"Ouch." Eddy grinned.

"He's not wrong." Samantha laughed as well.

"You could have told me this was going to be such a swanky event." Eddy glanced past him, through the glass double doors that led into the ballroom.

"Sorry I didn't give you all of the details. But we should get inside before it gets too crazy. Once the alcohol starts flowing things get a little wild."

"Wild?" Samantha stared at the gathering of well-dressed people inside. She couldn't picture any of them getting wild.

"We'll just drop off our coats, and meet you in there." Eddy nodded to the woman behind the coat check counter as Colin walked through the double doors. Then Eddy turned and helped Samantha out of her coat.

"Thanks." Samantha smiled as he gathered her coat. She was impressed by the suit he wore. It was black with gray pinstripes and he paired it with a gray tie and a white button up shirt. He looked handsome, in a way that she didn't expect. She got so used to his normal style, which usually involved wearing an old light-brown suit, that she forgot that he could dress up, too. Of course, his hat remained perched on the top of his head. As he took her arm she noticed that he carried himself with a certain level of confidence that she didn't see in their day-to-day life. She guessed it was because he'd stepped back into the role he was most familiar with. For this night at least, he wasn't retired.

"Looks like the entire police force is here," he mumbled as they moved through the doors. He saw many familiar faces, and many more that belonged to strangers. A pang of nostalgia carried through him as he realized that he was on the outside looking in now. In some ways that was a relief, but in the biggest way, it was a heavy blow to his self-image. He was still attempting to redefine who he was without a badge on his belt.

"Do you think there's anything to those rumors about Hank's less than stellar behavior?" Samantha followed his lead as he approached a table where Colin sat, a man on either side of him.

"I can't say for sure." Eddy lowered his voice as they neared the table. "There was once a time when I would have insisted that any bad word said about him was false, but experience has taught me that there are no certainties when it comes to people. Time can change everything." He pulled out a chair for her.

As she settled in it, she noticed that the men on either side of Colin sat rather close. Most men didn't intrude on each other's space. While women might lean close, touch shoulders, even whisper to one another, generally men left a safe distance. But these men were close enough to breathe down Colin's neck.

"Ah, Eddy, I was just talking about you." Colin grinned. "Do you remember Mitch and Riley?"

"Mitch and Riley?" Eddy squinted at them as he sat down beside Samantha. "Wait a minute, they can't be?"

"That's right. Hank's boy and his friend. All grown up." Colin chuckled. "And they are managers at the furniture factory on Main, now."

"Eddy." The older of the pair raised an eyebrow. "How are you, old man?"

"Can't be that old, if he has a date this pretty." The younger man winked at Samantha.

"Oh yeah, you're Hank's son all right." Eddy rolled his eyes and laughed. "Your father always was a charmer. You guys were always inseparable, looks like that hasn't changed."

"Do you remember that time you busted us, Eddy?" Mitch met his eyes. "Caught us at that party?"

"I remember." Eddy nodded. "Maybe we shouldn't talk about that."

"Great night." Riley smiled. "We were getting

along with some girls and were just about to score some drugs and then these two show up and break up the whole thing!" He groaned.

Samantha pasted a smile on her lips. She was used to boy talk, but that didn't mean she enjoyed listening to it.

"Listen, you never should have been there in the first place. Only fifteen, what were you thinking?" Eddy shook his head, his eyes heavy as they shifted between the two of them. "But I guess you're straightened up now, huh?"

"Only because you let us slide." Mitch picked up his beer and held it in the air towards Eddy. "We never would have gotten anywhere with a record."

"Never mind that." Eddy waved his hand. "You should be celebrating with your dad. Where is he anyway?"

"Eh, he's always running late." Mitch shrugged. "One of these days he'll realize the world doesn't revolve around him."

"Right, when will that be?" Riley chuckled.

"According to him the sun doesn't rise, unless he does," Mitch said.

"Giving the old man a hard time?" Colin's eyes widened. "Sounds like sour grapes to me."

"No sour grapes. He is just a tough taskmaster."

Mitch rolled his eyes. "Trust me, he's harder on me than he is on the officers under his command."

"Command?" Eddy looked between them. "I didn't realize he'd been promoted."

"Sure, he's a chief now, of 54th division." Mitch coughed. "Apparently, they have the highest records of jaywalking tickets and dog poop complaints. Real tough area."

"Easy now." Eddy wagged a finger at him. "Your father worked hard to get where he is, he deserves a little vacation in an easy division."

"To Dad." Mitch raised his glass in the air again. "And to Eddy, the man that saved our tails from being skinned."

"I'll drink to that." Riley laughed as he raised his glass as well. Colin joined in the toast as they all laughed together.

"Thanks, boys." Eddy nodded.

Mitch stood up, then rested his hand on Colin's shoulder. He leaned close and murmured something in his ear.

Colin's body tensed as he looked up at Mitch, who was at least fifteen years his junior. "You're mistaken."

"No, we're not." Riley stood up as well, straightened his collar, and stared hard into Colin's eyes. A second later they both turned and walked away.

Eddy watched them head towards the table in the front of the room where Hank was now sitting. He glanced from them, to Colin, and noticed that his friend's cheeks were bright red.

"Colin, what was that about?"

"It's nothing." Colin cleared his throat, then adjusted his position in his chair. "They're not the innocent kids they used to be."

"Were they ever innocent?" Eddy chuckled, then shook his head. "Those two were twin troublemakers, always making Hank sweat. At least I imagined he would be sweating. I don't think I've ever exchanged more than a few words with him."

"No, he wasn't very interested in getting in the middle of the affairs of his son and Riley. However, he was quick to demand favors to keep their names out of the system." He pursed his lips.

"Yes, I remember. You wanted me to book them. You got pretty upset with me back then." Eddy eyed him for a long moment. "Are you still upset with me about it?"

"No, you explained to me that if we weren't the ones to let them go, then someone else would be. Then you lectured them for two hours. I think I would have rather been in jail overnight than sit through that." Colin grabbed a beer from a passing tray. The waitress paused and offered Eddy and Samantha a drink as well.

"Thank you." Samantha smiled as she grabbed a glass of champagne. "Well, to be honest different countries, even different states within our own country have different juvenile policies. It's hard for me to imagine a child being put in jail. They haven't fully learned the impact their actions have, or the consequences they might face because of them."

"You can say that all you want, but it's not always so black and white." Eddy frowned as he took a sip of his beer.

"He's right, it's not. But trust me, if I hadn't listened to Eddy's advice on letting those boys slide, I might not still have a job." Colin clapped Eddy on the back. "You saved my skin that night, and many other times since."

Their conversation was interrupted as a cake was wheeled past them towards the front of the room. Samantha's mouth watered when she saw the marbled cake, topped with bright blue frosting. She absolutely loved cake, and even if Eddy had not invited her, she probably would have asked him to try to bring her a slice. She picked up her fork, in anticipation as the entire room erupted in song. She joined in, though with everyone standing, she couldn't see the man at the front of the room that they sang for. She didn't care too much, as her main interest was getting a piece of that cake.

CHAPTER 4

*E*ddy pushed his fork into his cake and took a bite. He had to admit it was very good. But his mind was on Colin, who didn't even pick up his fork. He kept glancing over his shoulder, though Eddy couldn't place exactly who he was looking at.

"Colin, what has you so shook up?" Eddy shook his head. "I've never seen you so jumpy."

"Eddy, I've gotten myself into something. I don't think there's a way out." He lowered his eyes and winced at the same time. "I just need you to know, I wouldn't go back and change any of it."

"Colin, tell me what you're talking about." Eddy's heartbeat quickened as he sensed his friend was genuinely afraid.

"I can't." He looked over his shoulder again, then back at Eddy.

"Colin, you invited me here for a reason." Eddy shifted closer to Colin's chair and tried to meet his eyes. "I know it wasn't just for champagne and birthday cake. Why don't you tell me what this is all about?"

"No, it wasn't. But we can't talk about it here. I'll tell you later. Right now, I just want you to keep your eyes and ears open. I want to have your unbiased opinion." He finally picked up his fork, and after a bite, he forced a smile. "Plus, this cake is really good."

"Yes, it is." Eddy took the last bite of his, then eyed Samantha's plate to see if she had any left. It was polished clean, too.

"Best I've ever tasted." She wiped her lips with her napkin. She'd been pretending not to listen to their conversation, but she'd heard every word. Curiosity coursed through her as she wondered what Colin was too nervous to talk about. Before either man could say another word, a hush fell over the crowd. Heads turned in the same direction, as a tall, slender man walked towards the stage.

Samantha had seen pictures of Hank when she researched him, but his presence still startled her.

He had a sense of authority that exuded from him in nearly visible waves. When he took the podium, the entire room became instantly silent. She even rummaged in her purse to make sure that her ringer was off. His hawk-like eyes swept the audience as he straightened his shoulders into a perfect line.

"Welcome, everyone. I'm touched that so many people wanted to come out tonight, to celebrate, me." He grinned. "Or was it just the free booze?"

Laughter flooded the audience. Samantha shifted in her chair. She looked over at Eddy, who seemed to be fixated on the man, just as everyone else in the crowd was.

Hank gave a short speech, packed with inside jokes, and stories about his heroism. He had the entire room hanging on every word. Samantha found herself swayed into believing that he was as impressive as he seemed to think he was.

"There he is, the man of the hour." Colin took a swig of his drink and closed his eyes briefly. When he opened his eyes again, Eddy was staring into them.

"It's about him, isn't it?" Eddy held his gaze. "Colin, what have you gotten yourself into?"

Just then the audience erupted in applause. Hank took a small bow, then walked away from the podium. As he eased his way into the crowd of people waiting to greet him, Samantha thought he looked like a famous actor, smiling at his fans.

"Meet me outside in ten minutes." Colin stood up from the table. He picked up the slip for his coat, adjusted his tie, then turned and walked away.

Eddy stared after him, uncertain what to think. The idea that he was being so elusive about why they were meeting, and somehow involved one of the most well-known law enforcement officers in the area, made him very uneasy. He wiped his mouth with a napkin, then stood up to follow him. An instant later he noticed Samantha beside him.

"Maybe you should stay here." He tilted his head towards the table. "I'm not sure what he's going to have to say."

"I'll stay out of the way if he wants to talk to you alone, but he said to meet him in ten minutes, where are you headed?" Samantha offered him a knowing smile. She had gotten to know Eddy so well that she could almost predict his actions.

"To say hello to a man I barely know and wish him a happy birthday." Eddy turned his focus back to Hank, who was surrounded by well-wishers. "I want to look into his eyes for myself. Colin is going to have quite a story to tell, I'm sure of it. I want an idea of what I'm getting into before I speak to him."

"Do you really think all of this is about him?" She raked her eyes over the man in the middle of the crowd.

"I don't know what to think, but I hope to find out every detail soon. Do you want to meet him with me?" Eddy smiled as he offered his arm.

"No, I learn more from observing than interacting, sometimes. I'll keep an eye on things from here. Just try not to block my view." She walked back towards the table.

Eddy bit back a retort about him blocking her view, he wanted to stay focused on the matter at hand.

When he walked up to Hank, he had to wait a few moments to get his turn to greet him.

"Well, well, if it isn't the famous Eddy." Hank laughed and clapped him on the shoulder rather roughly.

Eddy was too stunned to complain. He had no idea that Hank knew his name, let alone considered him famous. He cringed as he wondered what that might really mean.

"I'm sorry, I'm not sure that we've ever met."

"No, I don't think we have." He thrust his hand

towards him and Eddy accepted it with a firm shake. "But I have heard plenty about you. From Mitch and Riley, and Colin of course."

"Colin? Yes, I worked with him. I wasn't aware that you two knew each other well." Eddy furrowed a brow.

"Sure, we do. He's been one of my go-to guys for years now. Thanks for training him so well. And thanks for keeping the boys out of trouble. That kind of thing is frowned upon now of course, but back then rules and regulations were a bit looser, eh?" He grinned.

"I suppose, though I've heard that you're not afraid of a little rule bending." Eddy gazed at him from beneath his bushy eyebrows.

"If all ends well, then no harm done, right?" Hank gave him another clap on the shoulder. "I'm glad you could make it, Eddy. It's nice to see a fellow old man. Being surrounded by all of these young police officers just reminds me how old I am."

"You're a lot younger than me, but I'm glad I could restore your faith in your youth."

"Best birthday present ever." He grinned. "Make sure you have a good time." He turned and walked away.

Eddy stared after him. It wasn't unusual for an

older cop to make comments about the good old days, how things were done before regulations were tightened. That didn't alarm him. But if he and Colin were so close, why hadn't Colin mentioned it? What exactly did he mean by calling Colin his go-to? There was only one way to find out.

~

From where Samantha sat, she could see Eddy and Hank interacting. She detected a dominance in Hank that didn't surprise her. Powerful, confident men tended to puff out their chest just a little, and managed to look down at the person they spoke to, even if they were a bit shorter than the other. That wasn't an issue for Hank, as he was a good six inches taller than Eddy. His shoulders were rounded and relaxed, but his expression was vivid and determined. He led the conversation, both in voice, and in body language, and Eddy followed right along. This was a little surprising to her as Eddy tended to take the lead in conversations. Seeing him back down from the man by edging a step aside, made her wonder if he wasn't more than a little intimidated by Hank, or maybe he was doing it for another reason.

As Samantha watched Eddy walk away she was certain that he was going outside to meet with Colin. As tempting as it was for her to be there for that conversation, she knew it would be better to let them speak alone. If Colin was so concerned about someone else overhearing, she doubted he would welcome her, someone he didn't know, into the conversation. She turned her attention to her champagne and people watching. As minutes slid by she noticed that there was always a certain amount of space around Hank. Even when people gathered around him, they remained at a safe distance.

Samantha's thoughts were interrupted when someone set another glass of champagne down on the table. However, it was tilted when it was released, so the entire glass spilled across the table and into her lap.

"Oh no!" She jumped up as the liquid soaked through her skirt.

"I'm so sorry!" The man who had set down the glass, gasped and blushed. "I can't believe I was so stupid. Here, let me get that for you." He grabbed one of the cloth napkins off the table, which caused her glass of champagne to spill as well. "Oh no!" He groaned and thrust the napkin at her. She took it and wiped at her skirt. As she glanced up at him she noticed that he was familiar.

"Aren't you the doorman?" Samantha raised an eyebrow.

"Yes, I am. I'm also the biggest idiot in the world. I'm so sorry. Please forgive me." He grabbed her another napkin and offered it to her. "I just wanted to offer you a glass of champagne, and I've turned everything into a mess."

"It's all right, these things happen." Samantha gritted her teeth. She really liked the dress she wore, and was a bit upset that it had champagne all over it. But she knew it was just an accident and didn't want to give him a hard time about it.

"I'm sorry. My shift just ended, and the party host said that the staff is allowed to have some of the cake and drinks. I noticed you sitting here all alone, and I thought maybe you would like to share a drink with me. I guess not now." He chuckled, and blushed. "Let me give you my card, so you can send me a bill for the dry cleaning."

"Don't worry about that." Samantha smiled as she looked him over. She hadn't even noticed when he held the door for her that he was about her age, and rather handsome at that. There was something about the way he looked at her, with utter confidence, despite the way he stumbled over his words, and looked a bit like a fool. She wasn't there to meet anyone new, but she had no idea how long Eddy would be caught up with Colin. "If you get us two fresh glasses I'd love to share one with you."

"Really?" His eyes widened. "You're not upset about your dress?"

"It's just a dress." She shrugged.

"I'll be back in just a moment then." He held her gaze for a few seconds, then hurried off to the bar.

Samantha continued to wipe at her dress until she had most of the champagne out of it. She couldn't get it completely dry, but at least she might get a new friend out of it. After a quick glance at her phone to check the time, she looked towards the doors that led out to the parking lot. It was impossible not to wonder what the two men were discussing. She hoped that Eddy would be willing to fill her in, or her curiosity might just cause her to burst. When the doorman returned with their drinks, she was glad to have the distraction.

"Thank you." Samantha accepted the glass. "I'm Samantha by the way."

"Pete." He nodded as he sat down beside her. "Well, Peter if you want to be technical about it. But never Petey, got it?"

"Got it." She laughed. "I'm glad that you were able to join the party."

"Whenever the cops have a party here they invite all of the staff to join in. It's real nice of them." He took a sip of his champagne. "Where's your boyfriend? I don't want to step on any toes."

"We're just friends, very good friends. He's around here somewhere." She smiled. "I'm sure he'll be back soon."

"Crazy to leave a lady like you all alone." He lifted his glass to her. "To new friends."

"Yes, to new friends." She clinked her glass against his. "This hotel is so nice. Have you worked here long?"

"Not too long. It's just a way to fill my day at this point. I retired last year, and needed something to keep me occupied." He lowered his voice. "I'm a bit of a people watcher, so this is the perfect job for me."

"Me, too." Samantha laughed. "I could sit in one spot for hours and just watch all the people walk by. I like to imagine their stories."

"Maybe you should tell me yours." He gazed into her eyes. "I'm sure it's quite an interesting one."

"I've had my share of adventures." She raised an eyebrow. "Have you?"

"Oh, a few." He grinned.

Samantha found herself dazzled by the way he spoke to her. His voice was both warm and deep, it lulled her into a state of comfort and intrigue. Each time he spoke, his eyes contradicted what he had to say. She was fairly certain that he was toying with her, but she hadn't figured out why. When she checked the time on her phone again, she realized that almost thirty minutes had gone by from the last time she'd checked. Her heart lurched. What if Eddy was in trouble and she'd been too distracted by Pete to realize it?

"I'm sorry, I've enjoyed our conversation, but I have to be going." Samantha stood up from the table.

"Oh, far too soon." He frowned. "I really enjoyed getting to know you, Samantha. Perhaps we could try this again sometime?"

"I'd like that." Samantha nodded, then looked towards the doors again. "But I really should get going."

"Here, take the card so you can contact me if you change your mind about the dry cleaning." He dropped the card into her hand. "Could I have your number? So I can call?" He pulled out his phone.

Samantha hesitated. As a rule, she didn't often

hand out her number. In her experience it was a bad idea. Eddy reiterated that by always reminding her to be cautious. But she really did want to see this man again, and she didn't have time to debate it in her mind. She rattled off her phone number to him, then waved as she headed out the door. She stopped by the coat check for her coat, then spotted Eddy outside on the front walkway. As she stepped outside, a cool breeze struck her.

"Eddy? Are you still waiting for him?" She frowned as she buttoned up her coat. "I thought you would be done by now."

"He hasn't shown up." Eddy narrowed his eyes. "It's been nearly a half hour. Did you see him inside?"

"No, I haven't seen him since he left the table. Maybe he changed his mind?" She reached out and touched his hand. "Oh Eddy, you're so cold, you shouldn't be standing out here."

"I'll be fine." He pushed her hand away gently. "I need to find Colin. I've texted him numerous times, but he's not answering me. I tried calling, and nothing. I don't know what is going on here." He shoved his hands down into the pockets of his trench coat. As he did, he felt something strike his fingertips. He frowned as he fished out a small, brown paper bag. "What's this? I didn't have anything in my pockets."

"Maybe you forgot about it?" Samantha shrugged and rubbed her hands together. "Let's go back inside, it's getting chilly out here. Maybe we can find Colin."

"What is this?" He stared at the bag as if he didn't even hear her words. "I know this wasn't in my pocket." He started to open the bag.

"Eddy!" Samantha gasped as a rush of people suddenly pushed out through the front doors. She drew him out of the way just before he would have been caught up in the crowd.

"What is going on here?" Eddy shoved the bag back into his pocket. "Can someone tell me what's happened?" He searched through the faces of the people that fled the hotel. One of the waiters paused beside him and spoke in a low voice.

"Someone was found dead in the kitchen. The police are evacuating the building."

"Found dead?" Eddy grasped him by the elbow. "It wasn't an accident, was it? Or they wouldn't be evacuating."

"No, it definitely wasn't an accident." The waiter's face grew pale as he spoke, then he turned and continued on with the crowd.

CHAPTER 5

*E*ddy's mind swirled at the news that someone had been murdered.

"We need to get inside." He grabbed Samantha's hand and began to steer her around the side of the hotel.

"Do you think that's a good idea?" Samantha frowned. "What if we get caught?"

"You can stay out here, Sam, but Colin invited me here for a reason. This might just be it."

Samantha followed right behind him. There was no chance that she would let him go in there alone. When Eddy looked back and saw her there, he was both relieved and nervous. Relieved that he had some back-up he could rely on, and nervous that he would get them both into trouble.

"This way." He pointed down a side hallway.

"How do you know?" She matched her pace with his as they continued down the narrow hallway.

"All of the police are headed this way, so this must be where the body is." He gestured to a few patrol officers who were already near the end of the hall.

Samantha's stomach twisted as she wondered if the officers would notice them. However, they turned the corner without ever looking back. As they reached the corner, Samantha peeked around it.

"Wait a second." Eddy placed his hand on her shoulder. "I think we're near the kitchen. I can smell the food." He sniffed the air.

"How are we going to get any closer with all of these officers in the way?" Samantha whispered as she hung back, close to the wall. She knew if the officers saw them they would be kicked out of the hotel, and there would be no chance to find out more about what happened. Eddy seemed to be at a loss. "I'll get you in." She patted his shoulder, then stepped out into the hallway.

The moment she did, the officers noticed her.

"Ma'am, we're evacuating the premises, you need to leave." One of the officers stepped forward and pointed down the hallway to the exit.

"Oh, but I left my phone inside, I just need to grab it. I'm a doctor, and I can't be without it. I happened to be in the restroom when the evacuation started. I just need to get back into the ballroom to grab it." She looked between the men that stared at her. "How much harm could that really do?"

"You're really a doctor?" One of the officers eyed her.

"Yes." Samantha did her best to sound convincing and hoped that they wouldn't request proof. "I almost never leave my phone behind, but someone spilled champagne on my dress." She gestured to the stain on her skirt. "I rushed to the restroom to clean it off, and that's when the evacuation started. The officer that ushered me out of the restroom refused to let me retrieve my phone. I'm just hoping that you will see how important it is for me to have it back."

"All right, I'll take her." One of the officers tilted his head in the direction of the ballroom. "Can you two handle the final sweep?"

"Yes, we're on it." The two other officers headed

in the opposite direction down the hall. Eddy saw his opportunity as Samantha was led away by the third officer. He slipped around the corner and through the kitchen doors before anyone could stop him. The kitchen was quiet, but he could hear the chatter of police radios not far off. It was a very large space, and he guessed that the action was taking place somewhere else. He started to make his way forward. As he did, the side door of the kitchen that led to the ballroom abruptly swung open. Samantha stepped in, her face pale and her eyes wide.

"I think I lost him."

"Good job, Doc." Eddy winked at her. "Let's see if we can find out what's going on."

Eddy led the way towards the other side of the kitchen. Since they walked in from behind the main crime scene, most of the officers were facing in the other direction. Eddy stepped around a large butcher's block, and immediately froze.

"It's Colin!" He stumbled back, right into Samantha who stood just behind him.

"What?" She grasped his shoulder to steady him as she looked beyond him to the kitchen floor. A bolt of shock rushed through her as she recognized the figure sprawled out across the tiles. There was no question that foul play was involved, the crimson pool against the stark white tiles made that very clear. "Eddy, I'm so sorry." She pulled him close and wrapped her arms around him.

"What are you doing in here?" A voice behind her barked, causing her to jump.

Samantha and Eddy both turned to see Detective Brunner in the doorway of the kitchen. He looked at the other officers.

"I told you to clear the crime scene, so why are there two civilians in the middle of it?" His tone was sharp, and left no room for excuses.

One of the young officers cleared his throat.

"It's not his fault." Eddy straightened up and looked at Brunner. "I snuck in. We'll be on our way." He grabbed Samantha's hand and steered her out through the kitchen door.

"Eddy, wait!" Detective Brunner followed after him. "Did you know the victim?" He stared at him, his gaze unyielding.

"He was an associate of mine. But I didn't know him well. Good luck with your investigation, Detective."

Samantha started to draw away from him, uncertain as to why he wasn't telling the truth. She intended to tell the detective that they had shared a table with the victim, and he seemed to be involved in something that might have led to his death, but a sharp tug on her hand silenced her. She looked into Eddy's eyes, and saw the warning there. She didn't understand it, but she trusted him enough to heed it.

Once they were outside the hotel he turned to face her.

"We need to be careful what we say and to whom."

"Okay." She narrowed her eyes. "Even Detective Brunner?"

"Especially Detective Brunner. Colin wanted me here for a reason, he wanted to tell me something, and he didn't feel comfortable discussing it in a room full of cops. What does that tell you?" He lifted one of his eyebrows.

"That what he had to say involved someone in law enforcement?" Samantha's heart fluttered as a group of patrol officers walked past.

"Exactly. Until we figure out what it was that he had to say, we need to be cautious about what we say about any of this." He shoved his hands into his pockets again as a cold breeze carried through the parking lot.

"Eddy, this isn't just about a mystery that you need to solve. You've lost a very good friend."

Samantha gazed into his eyes. "You realize that, don't you?"

"Of course, I do." Eddy squinted as he grasped the bag in his pocket again. "What is this?" He pulled it out and opened the bag right up. The moment he did, he closed it again and shoved it back into his pocket. He grabbed Samantha by the elbow and steered her towards the car. "We have to get out of here."

Samantha noticed the urgency in his voice and it caused her heart to beat even faster. "What's wrong, Eddy?"

"Get in the car." He pulled open the door for her, and passed swift glances in all directions around the parking lot. "Hurry!"

Samantha slid into the passenger seat, her eyes wide and her mouth dry. If something had Eddy that shaken, she was sure it had to be quite serious. Once he was in the car beside her, he turned the engine on and drove out of the parking lot.

"Eddy, tell me what's going on. I'm involved in this, too, I have a right to know." Samantha grabbed the handle above her door as he took a hard right and she lurched to the side. "Slow down!" She growled her words.

He slammed on his brakes in an empty parking lot, then pulled the bag out of his pocket again.

"Look for yourself."

She was stunned as she noticed the quake in his hand. She pulled open the bag and discovered that there were a few stacks of hundred-dollar bills inside of it.

"What is this?" She gasped. "How did it get in your pocket?" She dug through the bag and found that there was a folded note in the bottom. "Did you see this?"

"I have no idea how it got there. It wasn't there when I went in, which means one of two things, someone is trying to frame me, or someone is trying to send me a message." He took the note from her and opened it up. "No, I didn't see this." His face grew pale as he read it over. Then he read it out loud.

'Eddy, in case something happens to me, this is what I wanted to talk to you about. It is evidence and there's a lot more where that came from. It will all make sense soon enough.'

"What does that mean?" Samantha narrowed her eyes. "Evidence of what? And who is the note from?"

"It must be from Colin." Eddy's forehead

creased as he considered the words. "He was obviously involved in some kind of investigation, I suspect into Hank Greer. But I have no idea what this money has to do with it, or how it can be used as evidence. He must have planned to tell me about it, but was worried that he wouldn't get the chance to. What I don't understand is how did he get this into my pocket?"

"He didn't." Samantha grabbed the sleeve of his trench coat. "The stain I saw today, the coffee stain, remember?"

"Yes?" He glanced at his sleeve.

"It's gone." Samantha ran her thumb over the place where it should have been. "I don't think this is your coat, Eddy."

"What are you talking about?" Eddy frowned. He took a closer look at the material and the way it fit the length of his arms. There was not a stain, and the coat was a bit small on him. "You're right," he murmured as he studied the coat. "It must be Colin's. I noticed he had a similar coat on last night when we were out for drinks." His voice trailed off. "I can't believe this. I can't believe he's really gone."

"I'm so sorry, Eddy, but we have to turn it in, and the paper bag that was in the pocket. If you don't, you're interfering with a murder investigation.

Well, I don't have to tell you the consequences of that, do I?" She locked her eyes to his.

"No, you don't." His gruff tone indicated that he might be a little annoyed that she mentioned it in the first place. "This is going to be messy." He sighed, then turned the car back on. "The sooner the better."

CHAPTER 6

*A*s Eddy drove back towards the hotel, Samantha placed a call to Detective Brunner. As she expected, it was sent to voicemail. He was in the middle of the initial stages of an investigation, she doubted that he would take anyone's calls at the moment. However, as they pulled back into the parking lot of the hotel, her cell phone began to ring. She was jolted by Detective Brunner's name on the screen.

"Hi, Detective Brunner, Eddy and I need to speak with you."

"About?" His voice was terse. "I'm in the middle of something very pressing, you know."

"Yes, I do. But this is important. Trust me. We're outside the hotel, where can we speak to you, alone?" Samantha scanned the front walkway. It was dotted with police officers and onlookers. There wouldn't be much privacy there.

"Meet me on the rear deck. It is completely cleared, but not being searched at this time." He hung up the phone before she could even agree.

Usually Detective Brunner was helpful, and patient, but today he seemed far from either of those things. She looked over at Eddy, nervously.

"He seems pretty upset. But he said to meet him on the rear deck. What are you going to tell him?" She frowned as he parked the car in front of the hotel.

"That somehow I stole a murder victim's coat, I suppose." Eddy stepped out of the car.

"You didn't steal it. The coat check gave you the wrong coat or maybe you and Colin got the tickets mixed up. They were on the table together." She joined him on the sidewalk.

"Splitting hairs. It's not going to matter. I'm going to be one of the first people they look at no matter what. I had no business being here." He led the way around the side of the hotel towards the back.

"Your friend invited you to a party, that's not suspicious."

"A friend that I hadn't spoken to in years. And then suddenly he's dead." His cheeks flushed. "No, Detective Brunner is not going to just let that go."

They reached the deck and Samantha spotted Detective Brunner as he stepped through the french doors onto the wooden planks.

"It's going to be okay, Eddy." Samantha remained at his side as he approached Detective Brunner with the coat in his hand.

"What is this about?" Detective Brunner crossed his arms as he looked between the two of them. "You know I can't have any interference in this investigation. A police detective murdered at a birthday party for a police chief? I am definitely going to be under the microscope here."

"I know." Eddy's expression was grave. "Colin was a good friend of mine."

"I'm sorry." Detective Brunner's expression softened as he studied Eddy. "I didn't know that."

"That's why I was here. He asked me to be here. He had something he wanted to tell me. I suspect it was about an investigation he'd gotten involved in. When I went to meet him outside to speak to him about it, I stopped and picked up my coat from the coat check. At least I thought it was my coat." He handed over the long trench coat. "Somehow they got mixed up."

"Somehow?" Detective Brunner raised an eyebrow. "You had nothing to do with the mix up?"

"No, nothing. I didn't even realize it was the wrong coat until I was in my car. Actually, Samantha was the one who pointed it out. But this was in the pocket." He held up the brown paper bag.

"You're telling me you didn't know that you got the wrong coat?" Detective Brunner took the paper bag from him.

"Look, Detective." Samantha flipped to a recent picture of Eddy on her phone, wearing of course, his favorite coat. "They're nearly identical. The coat check just made a mistake, or maybe Eddy and Colin got the tickets mixed up, or maybe Colin mixed up the tickets on purpose, so Eddy would get the paper bag. Maybe he knew he was in danger."

"I see." Detective Brunner nodded as he scanned the coat in front of him, and the coat in the picture. "So, what's in here?" He opened up the bag. When he saw what was inside his entire body tensed. "Do you know anything about this?"

"No." Eddy narrowed his eyes. "But I think it

has something to do with the investigation he was involved in." He glanced over at Samantha.

She received the message loud and clear. She was to be careful about what she said. The problem was, she wasn't great at following orders.

"We suspect it was someone with a badge." She raised an eyebrow. "Someone that might have even been here for the party. Maybe that's who went after Colin."

"Wait a minute." Detective Brunner held up a hand. "I think you're getting ahead of yourself. Eddy, do you want to tell me what Colin told you?" His heavy gaze weighed on Eddy's.

"He didn't have the chance to tell me much. I'm sorry. If I could help, I would." He frowned. "That's why I brought this in as soon as I found it. I'm sure if it has something to do with Colin's death you'll figure it out."

"I will." Detective Brunner swept his gaze along Eddy's face, then looked over at Samantha. "Did he say anything to you, Samantha?"

"No, not at all."

"Interesting." He rested his hands on his hips as he stared at both of them. "So, a man requested your presence, and help with potential police corruption, but he didn't tell either of you anything about it?"

"That's what happened." Eddy lifted his shoulders in a mild shrug. "You can believe us or not."

"Believe you? Do you think I have a reason to suspect that you're not telling me the whole truth?" He squinted at Eddy.

"No, sir." Eddy gazed back at him. "I'll answer any questions you might have."

"Good. Because I'm going to have some. Right now, I need to get these items logged into evidence. I'll be contacting you soon for an interview."

"I'll be available."

"We both will." Samantha nodded.

"What about my coat?" Eddy glanced towards the hotel. "Can I retrieve it?"

"Not now. I'll make sure it gets back to you." Detective Brunner grabbed the handle of the door that led into the hotel. "Rest assured, Eddy, whatever happened here, I will figure it out."

"I'm sure you will." Eddy watched until the door was all the way shut, then shook his head. "He doesn't have a clue."

"Unfortunately, neither do we."

Samantha fell into step with him as they headed back towards the parking lot. She noticed a tense silence exuding from Eddy. She could hear it in his sharp steps, the subtle clench of his jaw, and the way he kept his gaze pointed at the ground. It grew until they reached the car, when Eddy finally broke it.

"I just don't get it, Samantha." Eddy shook his head as he paused beside the passenger door.

"Don't get what?"

"How could you tell him that we suspected it might be a police officer?" He frowned as he jerked the car door open.

Instantly, Samantha realized that he was more than a little frustrated with her.

"I thought it was important information for him to have. I mean if someone would go after Colin don't you think it's possible that person will go after Brunner, too?" Samantha settled in the front seat. "I know you didn't want me to tell him, but when dealing with the police, especially their safety, I always err on the side of truth."

"Err on the side of truth?" Eddy sat down in the car and closed the door. "Did you think I intended to lie?"

"Well, you weren't being very forthcoming about it." She tilted her head to the side as she studied him.

"I didn't want him to know, because he is one of them. He could easily spread the word through the ranks, then whoever Colin was investigating will think that we're on to him or her." He buckled his seat belt, then started the car.

"Oops." Samantha bit into her bottom lip for a moment. Now that he'd explained it, she could see the value in keeping that information to herself. However, it still didn't change her opinion completely on it. "But I think Brunner needed to know, Eddy. He's involved in the investigation. He'll need any leads about who might have wanted Colin dead." She grimaced as she spoke. "I'm sorry, Eddy. I can't believe he's gone, and I barely met him. I know you two had so much history together. This has to be upsetting."

"People die." He grunted, then backed the car out of the parking spot.

Samantha didn't press him. Eddy kept his emotions close to the cuff, and she knew better than to try to force them out of him. He would open up, but he would do it at his own pace.

Silence filled the car for several minutes. Samantha realized that she had no idea where Eddy was driving to. He wasn't going in the direction of Sage Gardens, or any other place she was familiar with. After a few more minutes she realized he was just driving. She let it go, and relaxed in the seat beside him. If that was what he needed to do to work through some of his feelings she was happy to let him do it uninterrupted.

"We need to find out who did this." Eddy's hands tightened on the wheel. "Colin was on to something, something big, otherwise he wouldn't be dead. If only he'd told me what it was when I asked, we might have more of a head start."

"We'll just have to work with what we have for now." Samantha shifted in her seat. "We know it likely had something to do with money, since that's what he intended to give to you. But what?" She shook her head. "Maybe if we can get hold of his computer we could find some kind of record of what he was involved in."

"Maybe." Eddy nodded. He finally turned down a street that headed back to Sage Gardens.

"Did you take a picture of the note he left you? Maybe we can find more information in that."

"No, I didn't take a picture." Eddy glanced over at her, then back at the road. "I didn't need one."

"Why not?" Samantha narrowed her eyes. "It might have a clue hidden in it."

"I know that." Eddy parked in front of Samantha's villa. Then he reached into his pocket and pulled out the folded up note. "I have it right here."

"Eddy!" Samantha stared at him, then at the note. "That was evidence! You should have given it to Detective Brunner."

"It was addressed to me." Eddy shrugged. "No reason to hand it over." He turned in his seat to look directly at her. "What do you think would happen to me if Brunner found a note in Colin's pocket, addressed to me? I would become the main suspect."

"You don't know that. Detective Brunner admires you. He wouldn't automatically suspect that you were involved in Colin's death."

"Then he's not a very good detective. Because my first line of questioning would be directed at the person named on the note. I can't investigate or solve Colin's murder if I'm in lock-up, waiting for my chance to prove myself innocent, now can I?"

"I guess not." Samantha pursed her lips.

"I just wanted a little time to look into the note myself." He glanced through the passenger side window at her villa. "I'll wait until you're safely inside."

"Eddy, why don't you let me look into things with you?"

"I just need some time to myself to sort all of this out."

"Okay. But if you need me, I'm here."

"Thanks, Sam."

As she made her way up to her villa, she could feel his eyes on her. Normally, he would walk her up, he was such a gentleman, but she guessed his mind was too occupied. Either way, she unlocked the door, then glanced back, and saw him still waiting there. He would do anything he could to protect her, and she intended to do the very same.

CHAPTER 7

*E*ddy couldn't drive straight home, he needed to do something. Instead, he drove towards the one place that he and Colin always retreated to, to blow off steam. Eddy was drinking a bit more in those days, but he avoided cop bars. He didn't like the idea of being with cops all the time, he enjoyed having a break from them so he could clear his head. Instead he found an out of the way hole in the wall bar. He hadn't been to it in years, but he and Colin spent many nights there after tough days on the job. As he pulled into the parking lot he was relieved to see that The Bridge was still The Bridge. It hadn't been bulldozed or bought out by a trendy bar. Instead, its peeling blue paint still stood up against a worn parking lot. There were never more than a few cars parked in front of it, and tonight there was only one. The bartender would be in the back. Rex, if he still worked there.

The best thing about Rex was that was all Eddy knew about him, even after years of showing up at his bar. Rex wasn't a talker, which meant that Eddy didn't have to talk either, which meant that The Bridge became his haven. For some time, he resisted bringing Colin along, as he didn't want to share his haven. But after a particularly hard day, when he knew he couldn't let the rookie go off on his own, he invited him to the bar, and they shared their first beer together. It was a bonding moment, mostly because Colin confessed all of his fears and concerns about wearing the badge, and Eddy went out of his way to help him through them. There weren't many people, especially at that time in his life, that he spoke to for that length of time, or at that emotional level.

As he pulled the door open the familiar scent of stale beer and moldy nuts greeted him as if he'd only been there the day before. Never mind that he'd lost count of how long it had been since his last visit. There, behind the bar, looking only a few days older than the last time he saw him, was Rex. He rubbed a cloth over a glass, and didn't bother to look up.

Eddy sensed another pair of eyes on him, but they belonged to someone who would rather not be seen, seated in a booth towards the back. He ignored it, and sat down at the bar.

Only then did Rex glance up. He squinted at Eddy for a moment, then set down the glass he was only rubbing more smudges into.

"I know you."

"It's been a while." Eddy managed a small smile. "Beer, please."

"That's all we got." He shrugged as he placed a cold bottle on the bar.

"That's what I like." Eddy felt comforted that the brand hadn't changed. The place barely stayed afloat, and rarely had much variety in stock.

"Lucky you." Rex nodded as he turned his attention back to the glass.

"Lucky me," Eddy muttered to himself, and realized he'd made a mistake by coming there. Everywhere he looked reminded him of Colin. He reached into his pocket and pulled out the note that Colin left him. As he read it over, he knew there was no clue hidden in it. Colin said it would make sense soon enough, but he didn't know how. Colin left the note and money as a back-up, but he had intended to tell him everything himself. If only he'd pressed a little harder to find out faster, maybe he would know what happened, or maybe he could have prevented it. Instead he was stuck at a bar, with a useless note, and a bottle of beer that didn't taste as good as it used to.

Eddy tossed the note down on the table and sighed. Then he reached into his pocket and pulled out something else. He hunched his shoulders to hide it from view. It was a single one-hundred-dollar bill. He'd pulled it off the top of the top stack of money that Colin left in his pocket. He thought he might be able to find something out about the bill itself, and where it came from. But as he looked at it, he was surprised to see a few tiny symbols etched near the border of the bill. He knew that happened sometimes. It wasn't uncommon to see things scribbled on bills of any denomination. It was written too small for him to read. For a moment he wondered if they might just be smudges. But the edges were too defined to be random. As he leaned over it, he heard the footsteps of the bartender approach him.

"Need another?" He nudged the bottle of beer that was still half full.

"No, I'm good." Eddy didn't look up from the bill.

"I remember you coming in here. You and your buddy, right?"

Eddy looked up sharply.

"You do?"

"Sure. Two of my best customers." He hesitated. "Then you quit coming in."

"Yeah, our lives took us elsewhere." Eddy shrugged.

"Well, your life did." He eyed him for a long moment. "Colin said you retired."

Eddy sat back on the barstool and gazed at Rex with renewed interest. He had no idea that Colin continued to frequent the bar, or that Rex had known either of their names.

"I did." He pursed his lips as he wondered if he should tell him what happened to Colin. All at once, he had to. It was as if he had no choice. He'd never confided in a bartender in his life, yet today, he felt the need bubble up irresistibly. "Colin was killed today."

"What?" Rex took a step back from the bar. "Are you sure?"

"Yes, I'm sure." Eddy narrowed his eyes. "You'd gotten to know him pretty well?"

Rex looked towards the booth at the back of the bar, then turned his attention back to Eddy.

"You could say that." His voice wavered some. His hands balled into fists on the bar. "He was right."

"Right about what?" Eddy stared at him.

"He told me, if anything happened to him, that you would come in here. I doubted it. He said you hadn't talked in years."

"No, we hadn't, but he was right, I'm here." Eddy studied him skeptically, he couldn't think of a reason why Rex and Colin would be speaking about him.

"He was." Rex licked his lips, then looked towards the back booth again. When he spoke again his voice was barely above a whisper. "But why are you here?"

"I came in for a beer." Eddy picked up the bottle off the bar and took a long swallow. "I wasn't even sure this place would still be standing. I didn't expect you to still be here."

"I own the place now, actually." Rex raised an eyebrow. "It's not exactly a step up, trust me."

"Congratulations." Eddy nodded. "It's good to have your own business."

"I guess." He glanced towards the back booth again, then locked his eyes on Eddy. "Colin told me, if anything ever happened to him, and you came in here, like he knew that you would, I was to give you something. But I'm not sure if I should."

Eddy's mind began to mull over what Colin might have left him. Was it possible that his old friend would predict that he would return to The Bridge? He guessed it was, since generally he was a creature of habit.

"What is it?" He leaned forward some. He lowered his voice, because Rex had, though he wasn't sure why. He didn't overlook the way he kept looking over at the occupied booth. Maybe someone was there that he didn't want hearing the conversation.

"It's in the back. I'll show you." He gestured for Eddy to walk around the bar.

He stood up from the barstool and started to walk around the bar, but paused right at the edge. A ripple of caution carried through him. What if it was some kind of trap?

"Who is in the booth?" He looked into Rex's eyes, his expression hard.

"A customer." Rex stared back, just as sternly. "Let's go, it's back here." He pushed open the door that led into the back room.

Again, Eddy hesitated. He had no idea what Rex's intentions were. For all he knew, he could have had something to do with Colin's death. Still, if he wanted to figure it out, he would have to take some risks. He followed behind Rex. Once through the door they veered off into a small office. Rex stepped around behind the desk and pulled a key ring off his belt. He rummaged through the keys, then used a small one to open a lock on a drawer in his desk. Eddy watched, curious about what would come out of the drawer. It could be another note from Colin, or it could be a gun. He braced himself, ready to react.

"Here." Rex tossed something small and rectangular down on the desk.

"What's that?" Eddy stared at it.

"It's a flash drive." He raised an eyebrow. "Right, you're a dinosaur like me. It's a storage device, you plug it into a computer and you can access all of the files on it."

"I know what a flash drive is." Eddy sighed. "But what's on it?"

"I don't know. He just told me to give it to you if anything ever happened to him. He's dead, so now it's yours." He pushed the flash drive towards him. "I don't know what's on it. I never wanted to know. But—" He froze and looked past Eddy. "What are you doing back here?"

Eddy's heart dropped as he turned to face whoever was behind him.

Behind him was a short-statured man, with a thick, black mustache, and sharp, dark eyes. Although, he was petite in size, his attitude more than made up for it with confidence and authority.

"Am I interrupting?" He held up an empty glass. "I thought this was a bar, and I might be able to get a refill?"

Eddy quickly surmised that this was the man who had been sitting in the booth ever since he arrived at the bar. When he glanced back at Rex, he could see that the bartender had grown very pale. He watched the other man nervously.

"It's a private conversation, Orin. I'll be right out to get you another beer."

"Private, huh?" He locked his eyes on to Eddy's. "How can it be private, if it's about me? Don't you think I should be involved in the conversation if I'm the main topic?" He chuckled.

"You're mistaken, no one was talking about you. Orin, is it?" Eddy furrowed his brow. "I don't think I've ever met you before, so why would I have a conversation about you?"

"You didn't tell him?" Orin smirked as he spoke to Rex, but kept his eyes trained on Eddy.

"I didn't know if you would want me to. Colin told me to pass on the information, he didn't tell me to do anything more than that." Rex took a step back from his desk.

"So, Colin is dead, huh?" Orin scraped his nails back across the tight curls of his dark hair. "I can't say it surprises me. I warned him." He drew his lips into a thin line, released a long breath through his nostrils, then closed his eyes. "I guess I'll be the next to go."

"Please, can one of you explain to me what's going on here?" Eddy looked between them. "I know that you seem to have a lot more information than I do, but I can't keep up with all of this."

"You take a look at that flash drive, then we'll talk." Orin looked across the desk at Rex. "Did Colin leave you any cash for me?"

"No." Rex took another step back until he was against the rear wall of the office.

"Or did you just keep it?" Orin brushed past Eddy and headed towards Rex. "He told me, if something happened to him, you would have what I needed. So, where is it? I need to get out of town, if they offed Colin, then I'll be next."

"Calm down." Eddy placed his hand on Orin's shoulder. "I'm sure Rex is telling you the truth."

"Oh, you're sure of that, are you?" Orin turned swiftly to face Eddy. "I said, go home, and have a look at that flash drive, then contact me." He pushed a slip of paper into Eddy's hand. "We'll talk then. Until then, Rex and I have some business to settle."

"Orin, he didn't leave me anything, I swear." Rex looked between Orin and Eddy. "If he did I would give it to you."

"Well, then you're just going to have to front me the cash. I need to get out of here, and fast." He held his hand out to Rex.

"I don't have anything to give you!" Rex grimaced as Orin moved closer to him. "I swear!"

"Wait just a minute." Eddy grabbed Orin by the shoulder and pulled him back. "Now look, I don't know everything that's going on here, but I can tell you I'm not going to stand here and let you hurt this man. So, you better back off. Got it?"

"Oh, Mr. Tough Guy, huh?" Orin rolled his eyes. "Fine, but one of you had better come up with some money for me by tomorrow afternoon." He slammed his way back through the door and continued out of the bar.

"What is really going on here?" Eddy turned back to Rex. "Are you going to tell me now?"

"The flash drive will. I never wanted to be involved in any of this, but Colin and Orin didn't give me a choice. Eddy, you have to believe me, Colin didn't leave me any money for Orin." He rested his hands against the desk and drew in a few deep breaths.

"Who is Orin? You act like you're scared of him. What's the deal?" Eddy frowned as he studied Rex.

"I am scared of him. He's a horrible man. You should be scared of him too, Eddy. You know I almost decided not to give you the flash drive. I thought, you don't need this in your life. You don't need to get pulled into the middle of this. But Colin made me promise him."

"How was Colin mixed up with Orin?"

"I can't tell you exactly. But they would meet here. Orin thinks he owns me. Well, in a way, he does." He sighed. "I took a loan from him, biggest mistake of my life."

"I just don't understand, Colin was a great cop. Why would he be working with a loan shark?"

"Oh, Orin is far more than that." He tapped the flash drive. "Take a look. But once you do, you're not going to be able to get out of this." He held up his hands in the air. "Don't say I didn't warn you. Okay?"

"Okay, I guess." Eddy eyed him for a moment longer. "Are you going to be okay? Do you want me to stay while you close up?"

"I'll be fine." He shook his head. "Orin doesn't want me dead, yet. But be careful, Eddy. I told Colin he had no idea what he was getting into, and I'll tell you the same thing."

"Thanks. I appreciate the heads up." Eddy tucked the flash drive into his pocket, then headed out of the bar. Near the entrance he hesitated. He did a sweep of the parking lot to be sure that Orin was gone. The single additional car in the lot was no longer there. He wished he had paid more attention to it while it was still there.

CHAPTER 8

*E*ddy drove home, faster than he should have. He was eager to see what was on the flash drive, and also to look up information on Orin. If he was as dangerous as Rex indicated, then Eddy was sure that he would have a record. Another ding from his phone drew his attention. As he pulled into his driveway he noticed that it was from Samantha. He'd already ignored two texts and a call from her. He knew she was worried, and didn't want her to be concerned a moment longer. As he typed out a text, he wondered what the flash drive would reveal. He was apprehensive as he walked up to the door. He was tempted to invite Samantha to come over and view the drive with him, but what Rex said made him hesitate. It seemed as if once he saw what was on the drive, he would be a target. He didn't want to make Samantha one, too.

As soon as he was inside he turned on his computer and slid the flash drive into it. He rarely used the computer and it took him a few minutes to figure out how to actually access the information. Walt had explained it to him a few times, but when it came to computers, he tended to zone out. It was hard for him to recall exactly what to do. As he finally got the files open, his heart dropped. He saw documents, and photographs, and videos, of a few different police officers appearing to be taking bribes. It wasn't just one or two officers, it was a few. Which meant, the corruption had been going on for some time. To his surprise he found a document labeled 'Eddy'. When he opened it, he found a letter from Colin.

Eddy,

I'm sorry to leave this on your plate. I never intended to get myself killed, but if you're reading this, I did. It's not your fault. You were great to work with, and I never forgot how much you taught me. Not long after you retired Hank Greer took me under his wing. I thought it was great, until recently when I suspected that he was bending and breaking the rules. When I was going to arrest Orin Banks, he told me he had information on a crooked cop. I agreed to release him, if he told me the information. We've been working together ever since. I don't have enough proof yet, to implicate Hank Greer. I don't want to take down those involved without taking the head out. I hope you can do a better job than I did. You can't trust anyone, Eddy. Good luck.

Eddy read back over the letter. Part of him wanted to believe that it was a joke, but he knew that it wasn't. Colin was caught up in a web of corruption, and Orin was his informant. He grabbed his keys and headed out the door. There would be time to sort through everything later, but he had something he wanted to do first.

~

Samantha paced back and forth inside her villa. She realized her mistake of letting Eddy go off on his own far too late. He had just lost his friend, and she let him be alone? What was she thinking. She checked her phone again. After three texts and a phone call, he still hadn't responded. She'd walked down to his villa only to discover that he wasn't there, and neither was his car. Despite it being close to midnight, she followed the wide, well-lit path along the lake towards the main parking lot at the front of Sage Gardens. This was guest parking, and also overflow parking for people that had more than one vehicle, or just decided to park there for the night. She scanned the cars in the parking lot, but saw no sign of Eddy's car.

Now, back in her villa, she was certain that he'd gotten himself into some kind of trouble, already. What if he'd decided to hunt down Colin's killer all alone? As the time ticked by, her imagination ran wild with what could have happened to him. It was too late to call Walt or Jo. She knew they were both early risers, and she wasn't sure how they would react if she woke them without any valid reason. Eddy was a retired detective after all, he knew how to handle himself. He had the right to go anywhere he pleased, with anyone he chose, or alone. She knew she was overreacting just a little bit, but she still wanted to know where he was and what he might be doing. If only he would text her back, she could be put at ease.

Samantha sat down on the arm of her couch and closed her eyes. After a few deep breaths, she checked her phone again. There was still no call from Eddy. When her phone buzzed, she nearly dropped it on the floor. She sighed with relief when she saw it was a text from Eddy.

I'm fine. I'll update you in the morning. Get some sleep.

Samantha stared at the short text and pursed her lips. She wanted to find out more, but didn't want to bother him so headed to bed. One thing she was sure of, was that Eddy would need help to find out what happened to Colin. If she wasn't well-rested, then she wouldn't be much help. She crawled into bed, with many concerns still on her mind, not the least of which was just what Eddy might be getting himself into.

The next morning when Samantha woke up, she checked her phone first thing. There were no new texts or calls from Eddy. She sat up in bed and tried to decide what to do. She could call him, but if he was out late, she didn't want to wake him. After she had a cup of coffee and dressed, she decided to go for a walk. If she just happened to go by Eddy's villa, well that wouldn't surprise her, as he lived nearby. What if his car wasn't there? What would she do then? For all she knew he could have broken into Hank Greer's house and demanded answers from him.

As she approached his villa, her heart fluttered. It wasn't too farfetched for her to think that something terrible could happen to him, since just the night before, his friend had been killed at the same event they were attending. Someone was after

Colin, and if they saw Eddy there with Colin, then they were probably after him now, too, and maybe even her. She wasn't too concerned for her safety, but Eddy was the type that wouldn't back down from a challenge. She didn't want to find out that he'd gotten into a fight with the wrong person. Luckily, as she rounded the bend to Eddy's villa, she spotted his car right away. A wave of relief washed over her, as she approached his front door. She had promised herself she wouldn't bother him, but now she needed to see his face. As she knocked on the door, she expected that he might not answer. If he was sleeping, he might not hear her knock, and she wouldn't knock any harder than she was. However, an instant after her knuckles left the wood, the door swung open, and Eddy gazed out at her.

"Eddy, you look horrible." Samantha frowned as she studied the bags under his eyes, and the weary way his lips drooped at the edges.

"Sorry." Eddy shrugged. "Should I put something pretty on?"

"No jokes, I want to know what happened last night. Where were you?"

"Well, I want to tell you all about that. But first, there's something I need to show you. Come in." He stepped back from the door to allow her inside.

As she followed him she felt a rush of fear. She could tell from Eddy's demeanor that it was something big. Not much frightened him, but he appeared shaken. Perhaps that was just the lack of sleep.

"You didn't sleep at all last night, did you?" She frowned as she trailed after him to his computer.

"No, I didn't. Take a look at this." Eddy gestured to an assortment of files on his computer. There were photographs, open documents, and in particular a letter addressed to Eddy from Colin. As she read it over, her eyes widened.

"Oh no, Eddy, Colin really was into something serious."

"Yes, and now we both are, too. I wasn't sure if I should show you, but I knew you would never forgive me if I didn't. Samantha, I think Hank Greer was the head of all of this, but Colin didn't have the evidence to prove it, yet."

"Do you think he found out that Colin was investigating him, and killed him?"

"At his own birthday party?" Eddy shook his head. "I'm not so sure about that. It seems like a huge risk to take."

"Yes, it does." She narrowed her eyes as she

recalled Colin's reaction to Mitch and Riley. "Maybe, someone did it for him."

"Maybe." Eddy straightened up. "I went to Greer's house last night. I wanted to see what he was up to. But there was nothing out of the ordinary."

"Eddy, you have to be more careful than that." She frowned. "We need to let Jo and Walt help us with all of this. The more hands helping with the investigation, the more likely we can solve this."

"I don't know, do we really want to put them at risk?" He looked into her eyes. "I don't want you all getting involved."

"I think we should let them decide." Samantha pulled out her phone and sent a text to Jo and Walt asking them to meet up for an early lunch. She and Eddy spent the next two hours poring over the information on the flash drive. Although there was a lot of it, none pointed specifically to Hank, and none indicated who might have killed Colin.

CHAPTER 9

When Eddy and Samantha headed to Samantha's house to meet the others for an early lunch, they found Walt and Jo already waiting there for them.

"Sorry we're late." Samantha unlocked the door. "I'll get something simple and delicious together in no time." Samantha wasn't exactly a whiz in the kitchen, but she could make a delicious sandwich.

"Great." Jo patted her stomach. "I'm a bit hungry. I'll help you."

The two women stepped into the kitchen while Walt and Eddy settled at the dining room table. Samantha glanced at Eddy. She knew he hadn't decided whether to involve his friends yet or not.

Walt seemed to sense that something was up. He kept prodding Eddy for information.

"Walt, enough," Eddy snapped at him. "I had a rough night, okay? I didn't sleep."

"Sleep is vitally important for the health of the human body, not to mention what sleep deprivation can do to your mental health." Walt frowned. "There's no excuse for missing out on a good night's sleep."

"Walt, please." Eddy locked eyes with him. "Enough."

"What's going on with Eddy?" Jo leaned over the counter, closer to Samantha as they made sandwiches. "I've never seen him like this."

"His friend, the one who invited him to that party last night was killed. At the party." Samantha sighed.

"Oh, that's terrible. From the way he spoke about Colin I know he cared for him. I can't believe this happened." Jo shook her head. "Well, of course we'll have to figure out who did this to him. We can't take the chance that the police won't figure it out."

"Thanks." Eddy glanced up at them, he had caught Jo's last few words. "I really appreciate that, Jo. But this situation is a bit more dangerous than I expected. I want you both to really think about this before you decide whether you want to help or not."

"Hey, we have to look out for each other. Right?" Jo sat down at the table with him.

For a few minutes they exchanged information about what happened at the party, then Eddy rested his hands on the table and looked at each of them in turn.

"Look, I really do appreciate all of you wanting to help me out with this, but it's important that you understand what you're getting into here. This isn't just a death, it was a murder, and whoever Colin was investigating probably had something to do with it. If we investigate this, we could all be at risk, and I don't even know who to watch out for."

"But if we don't investigate it, then Colin's killer might never be found." Samantha rested her hand on top of Eddy's. "I'm going to help you in any way that I can."

"So am I." Jo nodded as she smiled at Eddy. "I'm up for anything anybody tries to throw at me. I've got your back, buddy."

"Thanks." Eddy met her eyes and smiled in return.

"Let's try and think about this logically." Walt's brows knitted as he looked at Eddy. "Your friend was trying to tell you about something, something that likely got him killed, and now you want to investigate what that was, making yourself a target?"

"Eh, that's about right." Eddy frowned.

"It doesn't seem like a wise thing to do." He shrugged. "But I've learned that friendship isn't very logical. I'm willing to help however I can."

"That means a lot to me, Walt. Honestly, I'm not sure what we can do. I have a lot of information but very little direction. And there's one other thing." He looked around the table, then specifically at Samantha. "I met Colin's informant last night. From what I can tell he is a very dangerous man. His name is Orin Banks, and I'm not sure that I'll be able to keep him out of this investigation."

"Orin Banks, I'll see what I can find out about him from my contacts." Samantha pulled out her phone, walked out of the room and placed a few calls. After a few minutes she walked back in. "Oh, this doesn't look good at all. He has a long criminal history."

"I know." Eddy frowned. "He might have the information that we need, but I'm not willing to overlook the idea that he might have also been the one to kill Colin."

"Stabbed in the back by a snitch?" Jo scrunched up her nose. "I could see that happening."

Eddy opened his mouth to speak, but he was silenced by the sound of his phone ringing. He checked the screen, then frowned as he looked up at the others.

"It's Detective Brunner. I'm sure he wants his interview." He placed the phone to his ear. "Hello?"

"Eddy, I need to speak with you. Can you come into the station?"

"Sure, what time do you want me there?" He pushed down the uneasy feeling in his stomach. Why did they have to meet at the station? What had Detective Brunner found?

"As soon as you can get here. I've got a lot to get accomplished today, and I'd like to start with you. Please come alone, I want to speak to Samantha separately."

"Okay. I'll be there soon." Eddy hung up the phone, and stared at the screen for a moment.

"He wants you to come in now, doesn't he?" Samantha reached for her purse. "I'll go with you, we can get both of our interviews done at the same time."

"No." Eddy narrowed his eyes. "He wants to

speak to us at separate times. He asked me to come alone, as soon as I can."

"What do you think he's up to?" Samantha frowned, then glanced at the others. "Anyone?"

"He's conducting normal interviews, that's all." Eddy cleared his throat. "It's normal procedure. It's easier for him to separate our accounts if he takes them on separate occasions. I'm sure it's nothing."

"You don't sound sure." Walt narrowed his eyes. "You only clear your throat when you're not sure of what you're saying, or you're trying to avoid something."

"Walt!" Eddy shot him a frustrated look. "Stop watching me so closely, it's creepy."

"Don't take it out on Walt." Jo rested her hand on Walt's shoulder. "He's only trying to help, Eddy, we all are." She met his eyes.

"You're right, I'm sorry." Eddy frowned as he looked at Walt. "Your observations are correct. I am worried that he might have a strong reason to want to meet with me at the station alone. I have no idea what he might have turned up, and that makes me nervous."

"Then let me go with you." Samantha stood up from the table. "You don't have to follow his directions, it was just a suggestion, right?"

"I'll be fine." Eddy smiled. "There's one more thing." He hesitated as he looked at Samantha. "The note wasn't the only thing that I kept." He pulled a plastic bag out of his pocket and placed it on the table. Inside was the hundred-dollar bill with the symbols on it. "I kept this from one of the stacks of money. It was on the top and it has small symbols written on it. I think they might be connected to the investigation. Maybe you three can take a look and see what you think?"

"You kept this?" Samantha looked from the bill, to Eddy. "Do you know how much trouble—"

"Yes." He stared straight into her eyes. "I didn't do it lightly. I just don't know who to trust. I'm not sure if Detective Brunner is impacted by all of this. You saw the files, there are police officers involved."

"He's been trustworthy so far." Samantha frowned.

"I know. It's just one bill, out of a few big stacks."

"Are you going to take it back to him now?" Samantha glanced at the bill on the table.

"No." Eddy straightened his shoulders as he looked into her eyes. "Not until we figure out what those symbols mean. Colin left me that for a reason, maybe it's because he thought I'd be the only one that could figure it out. If I hand it over to Brunner, we might never figure it out."

"Understood." Samantha looked back at the bill. "We'll keep searching to see if we can find out anything more about it. All right?"

"Thanks." Eddy swept his gaze over each of his friends. "Thank you all for your help, I mean that. I know, I don't exactly show it well, but I do appreciate it."

"We know you do, Eddy." Jo smiled at him.

Eddy gazed at them for one more long moment, then turned and headed out of the villa. As he walked back to his villa to get his car, the weight of the sleepless night struck him. He wished he had gotten some rest as he had no idea how he would hold up to Brunner's likely interrogation.

～

*A*fter Eddy left there was a heaviness in the room. It seemed as if no one wanted to be the first one to speak. Jo snatched up the bill to take a closer look.

"He's right, our best lead are these symbols. They were put here for a reason."

"I can do an image search and see what I can

come up with." Samantha grabbed her computer and brought it to the table. "Some businesses use symbols in their names, the money could be related to one."

"Good thought." Walt frowned. "I'd like to take a look into Orin a little bit further. Was there anyone else at the party that you thought might be involved in this. If Greer is part of this, I imagine some of his crooked friends were there as well."

"I'd agree with that." Jo narrowed her eyes. "The trouble is it's quite difficult to tell a good cop from a crooked one. It would be nice if they wore different types of badges, wouldn't it?"

"That would be pretty illogical." Walt eyed her for a moment. "It's hard to commit a crime when you're advertising your intentions."

"I know, it was a joke, Walt, sorry." Jo frowned. "No, they don't wear different badges, but in some circumstances they can be fairly easy to spot if you know what you're looking for. There's an easy tell if a cop is on the take. Nicer watches, nicer suits, new shoes. Most police officers, even detectives wear the same pair of shoes for years. If you see a cop with shiny shoes and a nice watch, he's more than likely on the take."

"That can't be true." Walt frowned. "Why would

anyone be that obvious? Wouldn't they take precautions to hide it?"

"You can't prove anything with watches and shoes. Plus, if a cop is on the take he's not that bright to begin with. It never ends well." Jo shrugged.

"She's right about that. It usually blows up in the end." Samantha tapped a few more keys on the keyboard as she sorted through search results. "But in this case, we may be looking at a much more systemic problem."

"Could be a very touchy situation. I think we need to find out more about this Hank Greer. I can help with that." Jo smiled as she glanced between the two of them.

"Wait a minute here, we're talking about a top cop, I don't think it's a good idea to go anywhere near him." Walt locked eyes with her.

"Oh, don't worry, I won't go near him. I'll just take a look around when he's not home."

"You seem a little eager to do this." Walt placed his hand over hers. "Perhaps you should evaluate why that is."

"Oh, I know exactly why that is. If Greer is a crooked cop, then I want to make sure he is taken down."

"Okay, let's just slow down." Samantha looked up from the computer. "I think I figured out what these symbols mean. There's a small property investment company in town, Sunny River Property Investments. It has these same symbols on its website." She turned the computer around to show them. "I think maybe this money came from that company."

"One of the workers was having art time?" Jo raised an eyebrow.

"No, I think maybe Colin drew the symbols on here. Maybe to denote where the money came from, maybe because he was bored waiting for a meeting. I have no idea why, but I think we should pay a visit to the investment company and see what we can find out."

"Sounds good." Walt nodded. "Let me look into the company a bit first, you two eat your breakfast. It's the most important meal of the day." He took over Samantha's computer and began looking for information on the company. "If it's as small and local as you say it should be fairly simple to get information on the company's—" He stopped short, then tapped a few keys. "Well, this is unusual."

"What is it?" Samantha peered across the top of the computer at him.

"I can barely find anything out about the company. For a business like that I would expect to find advertising and other basic company information at the least. Their website barely has any information on it."

"I think it's safe to say that if they don't offer much information about their company online, either they have a really bad marketing department or, they have something to hide." Jo finished the last bite of her food then pushed her plate aside. "We need to find out what it is."

"We're back to paying a visit. Walt, would you join me?" Samantha asked.

"Sure. I'm quite curious about this now and I doubt I'll be able to rest until I find out more about it. Jo, are you going to come along?"

"No, I don't think so. I have a few things to do in the garden. I'm sure that you two can handle this. But let me know if you hear from Eddy, okay?"

"Sure." Walt studied her closely. "You're not going to do anything reckless, are you?"

"Like break into an investment company?" Jo smiled sweetly. "Of course not, Walt. I'm reformed, remember?" She patted his shoulder. "No need to worry."

He watched as she headed for the door.

"Be careful, Jo."

"Always." She winked at him over her shoulder, then disappeared.

"Walt, don't worry, I'm sure she's just going to do some weeding." Samantha cleared the plates.

"I'm not sure about that. Not at all." Walt offered a grim frown. "So, how are we going to find out more about Sunny River?"

"Simple. Mr. and Mrs. Balin will want to invest in some property." Samantha bit into her bottom lip. "Do you think they will want to see a cash deposit?"

"Cash deposit?"

"Don't some investment places want some cash up front, like a deposit, before they look for investments for you. Since we can't use our real names, we can't use a check to do it, we'll need some cash." She finished washing the dishes then turned to look at him. "I don't have it. Money is tight for me right now."

"We should be okay." Walt nodded. "If they do require something, which I doubt they will, we can always delay them."

"Good." Samantha slung her purse over her shoulder.

"We need to take another look at your budget if

you're so tight. You should be putting money away." Walt stood up from the table.

"Yes, I know, but there was this sale."

"We've talked about this, Samantha." He smiled. "You're supposed to call me, remember?"

"I remember." Samantha sighed as she stepped out the door, then waited for him to join her. "But sometimes I don't want to remember."

"It always feels better to have a nest egg than to have a new blouse."

"Give me some credit, it was shoes." She grinned as she locked the door.

"Oh shoes, that makes it better." Walt rolled his eyes. "I know you too well for that, Samantha. What was it really?" He followed her towards her car.

"Okay, I might have made a few too many donations this month. It's just that people always have a cause, and what good is money if it's not doing some kind of good?" She unlocked the doors to her car and settled in the driver's seat.

"You're a good person, Sam." Walt buckled himself in beside her. "But you have to take care of you first."

"I'll work on it." She flashed a smile at him. "Shall we invest in some property, honey?"

"Absolutely, darling."

CHAPTER 10

*E*ddy sat outside the police station for a few minutes as he decided whether to go in. He was experiencing an incredible amount of conflict. With his history as a police officer, he knew how important it was for Detective Brunner to get the information that he needed. However, it was his freedom on the line, and he knew that he'd already done things that pushed the line of legal, not the least of which was keeping that one-hundred-dollar bill. When he finally climbed out of the car, his mind was still on the option of fleeing. But he noticed Detective Brunner in the lobby of the police station. He was a good man, and a good detective, there was no reason to suspect that he was corrupt. However, Eddy had seen great men taken down by greed. It started out small, but it snowballed fast. Was Detective Brunner one of those men?

Eddy was about to find out, because Detective Brunner spotted him, and pulled open the door.

"Eddy, thanks for coming in." Detective Brunner held the door open for him.

"Sure." Eddy stepped inside, then followed the detective down a hallway to a small office in the back of the station. Unlike an interrogation room, it had windows, and a desk. It felt more formal than he expected. Silently, he sat down across from the detective. If he'd learned anything while wearing a badge it was to keep his mouth shut when he might be in trouble.

"Wow, this whole thing is a mess." Detective Brunner shook his head. "Try explaining to the police commissioner that someone was murdered at a party full of police officers. Trust me, it did not go well."

"Sounds like a difficult situation." Eddy shifted in his chair.

"Yes, I would say that it was. Which is where you come in." He sat back in his chair and eyed Eddy with a half-smile. "Isn't it just my luck that one of the best men to ever wear the badge just happened to be at this party, too?"

"Hank Greer?" Eddy raised an eyebrow. "What does he have to do with me?"

"No, not Hank Greer." He narrowed his eyes. "I'm talking about you, Eddy. You were there the entire time, weren't you?"

"Me?" He chuckled. "Wow, you must really be desperate for information. Yes, I was there most of the time."

"Most of the time? Where else were you?" His eyes, hawk-like, remained fixated on Eddy.

"Like I told you before I was outside waiting to meet Colin, but he never turned up." He returned his gaze, just as steadily. "I was not in the hotel for some time. I did not go back in until the evacuation began."

"Okay, let me get this straight." The detective moved his pencil across the pad of paper in front of him, but Eddy could tell that he hadn't actually written anything down, he'd just drawn a line. Was that an indication that he was about to cross one? "When you saw everyone running out of the hotel, you thought it was a good idea to go back inside? Even though you were aware that the police officers wanted the building cleared?"

"Yes." He frowned. "I thought someone might need my help. I thought, my friend might need my help. You wear a badge, you know that the urge to help in a crisis doesn't just turn off."

"So, you went back in, to see if you could help?" He nodded. "But that still doesn't explain why you were outside in the first place."

Eddy stared hard at the man across from him. He knew that he had to make a decision now. He knew that Samantha would be asked the same question, and he imagined that she would answer honestly. So, the truth would come out eventually. If he refused to tell the truth now, then he might be faced with even more trouble later. But the important question remained. Could he trust Brunner? He was about to find out.

"I went outside to meet with Colin. He instructed me to wait ten minutes, then meet him in front of the hotel. I waited the ten minutes, then I went out to meet him in front of the hotel." Eddy folded his hands across his slightly rounded stomach.

"Did he tell you why he wanted you to meet him outside the hotel?" He studied him intently.

"As I mentioned before, Colin was involved in something, that may or may not have to do with the police. He said we couldn't discuss it there, with so many people around, so he wanted to speak to me privately."

"And did Colin ever meet you?" He made another note on the paper. This time, it looked like he was actually writing something. It occurred to him that Brunner might be trying to build a time-line. If that was the case, then they may not have been able to pin down the time of Colin's death.

"No, he didn't. It was approximately thirty minutes after we arranged to meet outside that everyone began to run out of the hotel." He eyed the paper. "So, it was approximately forty minutes after I'd last seen Colin. That doesn't leave a lot of time for a murder and to cover your tracks."

"It left enough, apparently." He looked up from the paper and met Eddy's eyes. "Thank you for working with me on this. You may very well be the last person that saw Colin alive."

"That's not possible." He narrowed his eyes.

"Why not?" Detective Brunner's tone became sharper.

"Because, I am not the one who killed him. The person who killed my friend, is the last person that saw him alive. Not me."

"I see." He cleared his throat.

"Sorry, Detective Brunner, your usual tactics are not going to work on me."

"I guess you have experience on your side." He set his pencil down.

"I have innocence on my side. I had nothing to do with Colin's death, and the more time you spend trying to pin this on me, investigating me, the less likely it will be that you solve this crime." He tapped his fingertip on the desk and looked into his eyes. "That is experience talking. It might be a good idea for you to listen."

"Maybe in all of that experience you discovered for yourself that when you have a difficult witness, it usually means they know more than what they're telling you." He laid his hands flat on the table. "You're not telling me everything, Eddy, and that means I need to keep my focus on you. If you'd like me to move on to a new suspect, then you should be more forthcoming. If Colin was really your friend, why wouldn't you want to tell me everything? That's what has me concerned, Eddy."

"Colin was my friend." Eddy stood up from his chair, though was careful not to appear threatening. "Don't question that. My friend, Colin, stumbled on to something that got him killed. He felt as if I was the only one that he could turn to. What does that tell you, Detective?"

"It tells me that you think I might be a crooked cop." Detective Brunner gazed up at him. "And I'm disappointed by that."

"Then prove me wrong." He slid his hand into his pocket and pulled out the small flash drive. He placed it on the desk between them. "Think hard about whether you want to look at the information on here, because once you do, you're not going to be able to back out."

"What's on it?" He picked it up and turned it between his fingertips.

"What Colin wanted to tell me, what I know about this."

"I'll take a look at it." The detective kept his gaze on him. "But I still need to talk to Samantha."

"Feel free." He shrugged.

"Eddy, I don't think I need to tell you that you need to be careful." He tapped the drive lightly against the desk. "If you know the same things Colin did, you could be in danger as well."

"I'm touched that you're so concerned." He narrowed his eyes. "You just do your job and find out what happened to my friend, who was a very good cop. All right?"

"I will." Detective Brunner stood up from the table and offered his hand. "I'll be in touch."

"Good." Eddy gave his hand a firm shake. "Watch your back, Detective."

"You too."

Eddy turned and left the office. Even as he approached his car he wondered if someone might rush him from behind and place him in handcuffs. Despite his lack of alibi, Detective Brunner hadn't seemed that suspicious of him. Was that because he trusted Eddy, or was it because he knew who the real killer was?

CHAPTER 11

*J*o ran her palm down along the snug, black shirt she wore. It matched the skin-tight, black pants she wore. Her long, dark hair was pulled back and tightly braided. One glance in the mirror told her she was prepared. One more check of the tools hidden on her belt assured her that she had everything she needed. As she left her villa she pulled a black baseball cap down low over her face. She walked away from her car in the driveway, then cut through the field between the lake and the parking lot. Even if she was spotted, no one would be able to recognize who she was. Once she was out of Sage Gardens she boarded a bus, careful to keep her face turned away from the camera in the corner. Twenty minutes later she stepped off the bus in a vastly different neighborhood.

Sage Gardens was situated in a suburban area, with a mixture of lower middle-class and middle-class families surrounding the retirement village. But the neighborhood she'd traveled to was filled with large houses stacked to the brim with all kinds of goodies that would be easy to fence. However, she ignored that lure. As a very skilled cat burglar she had committed her fair share of crimes, but only for the purpose of survival. Now she'd turned over a new leaf, and though she still felt a thrill as she made her way towards her target, her only goal was to help Eddy solve his friend's murder.

Jo lingered outside the gate that surrounded the large house. She was quite familiar with the gates of these types of neighborhoods. Sure, it looked like they were there for the sake of security, but they actually served very little purpose, other than to make the owner feel more important. They all wanted to be kings and queens of their castles.

The house itself was not difficult to access. A good guard dog would have made it much more of a challenge. Although there were plenty of cameras, they weren't motion censored and pointed at stationary spots around the outside of the house.

Glass sliding doors faced the pool on the rear patio. She knew she'd found her way in when she spotted them. They were the most vulnerable doors that she worked with. Most people forgot to lock them, or if they did, the locks were easily picked. Many times, they weren't alarmed, or if they were the alarm was often turned off, due to heavy traffic going in and out of those doors. She noticed that there was an alarm connected to them, but the red light that would signal it was active was turned off. However, the door itself was locked, at least she thought it was when she gave it a tug. But it moved just a little too much to be locked. She noticed a bar in the tracks of the door and rolled her eyes. She pulled a long, thin, silver tool out and slid it between the door and the house. Once it was underneath the door, it took a sharp shove to knock the bar out of place. As it rolled across the tiled floor beyond the door, she worried that it might draw the attention of someone inside.

There was no car in the driveway, but that didn't mean that there wasn't a maid or someone else in the house. She allowed a few minutes to slide by. When there was no sign of movement inside, she shifted her focus to the door again. Now that the bar was out of the way it easily slid open. She braced herself for the possibility of an alarm going off, but was greeted with silence. The interior of the house was spacious, well-kept, and not as well-decorated as she expected. Greer had money, but he didn't advertise it as much as those in his position would.

As Jo walked along the halls she noticed pictures that lined the walls. Most of them were of a boy, from infancy to adulthood. She guessed they were of the son Eddy had mentioned. Greer was in some of the pictures with him, but there was no evidence of a wife or mother. She guessed that Greer was divorced and he'd done his best to wipe the memory of his former spouse from his house. Was it once theirs? She glanced around again, but didn't notice any hint of a feminine influence. Maybe he became crooked after their divorce. Maybe that was the impetus that had set him off the path of honesty.

Jo decided to try his office first. That might be where he hid important details about his double life. She found it on the ground floor not far from the front door. When she began to shuffle through the paperwork on the desk, her heart rate spiked. She wasn't sure why. Maybe because she was in a police chief's home office, illegally, which could mean going back to prison for life. It occurred to her that she had put herself in a very precarious position without even much of a second thought.

"I must be bored." Jo sighed as she came across a locked drawer. She easily picked it, and inside were several stacks of cash. She tensed as she saw them. By her estimate there was well over one hundred thousand dollars in the drawer. That was not something that most people would leave in their office, not even in a safe. She snapped a few pictures, then froze.

If she wasn't mistaken that was the sound of the front door being eased open. Her heart caught in her throat as she eased the drawer closed. There was no window in the office, and nowhere to hide. There was no way to escape. She boldly stepped through the office door and discovered Hank Greer just inside his front door.

He gazed back at her without a trace of surprise in his eyes. She realized that somehow he knew she was there.

"Do you want to tell me what you're doing in my house?" He stared hard at her from across the room.

She couldn't ignore the gun on his hip. He had the right to use it. She had broken into his house.

"Take it easy." Jo raised her hands slowly into the air. "I'm not armed."

"I don't care if you're armed or not." Hank crossed most of the hall in three long strides, but still left some distance between them. "I want to know why you're here."

"Just looking for some cash. That's all." She continued to stare at him, not at his face, but at his shoulders, his elbows, and the curve of his relaxed fingers. She waited for the subtle twitch that would indicate he was about to reach for his weapon. It would give her less than a second to dive out of the way.

"Cash? Aren't you a little old for breaking into places?" Hank swept his gaze over her. "What are you, forty? Forty-two?"

She tried not to be flattered. It was not the type of situation where she should be.

"I didn't take anything. All right?" She forced a smile to her lips. "No harm no foul, right?"

"Plenty of foul." He took another step towards her, leaving only a few feet between them. "Do you know who I am?"

"Someone who likes large houses and doesn't like dogs?" Her hands still hovered in the air.

"Lady, you broke into the wrong house." He rested his hand on his hip, where the gun was hidden by the hem of his shirt.

"Call the police." She swallowed thickly. "Have me arrested."

"I don't think so." His lips curved into a slow smile.

The ice in his eyes sent a bolt of fear through her. He had no intention of calling the police.

"I didn't take anything. You can see for yourself. Nothing." A shudder carried up along her spine.

"What did you see?" He took another step towards her and looked into her eyes.

"Nothing. I didn't even have a chance to look around. You caught me so fast. I really did break into the wrong house." Jo kept her tone respectful, careful not to move, or give him any reason to draw his weapon.

"You're lying." He squinted. "And not well, either."

"I'd like to leave here alive. What is that going to take?" Jo focused on keeping herself calm, with steady even breaths.

"I'm not a murderer." Hank smiled. "But I don't like it when someone breaks into my home." He gestured to the front door. "Go ahead, leave."

Jo didn't move, only continued to stare.

"I'm not going to shoot you in the back." Hank's smile spread into a grin. "I don't need to. If you breathe a word about anything you saw between these walls, then you will pay the price. Understand?" His hand remained on his hip.

"Yes." Her heartbeat quickened as she realized he was actually going to let her go. She moved with cautious steps towards the door. It wasn't until she was outside, that she drew a full breath. She'd made it out alive, and free, but why?

CHAPTER 12

"I'm not sure that my tie is straight." Walt looked in the mirror, then shifted his tie again.

"You look great, Walt." Samantha checked her hair in the visor mirror, then flipped it closed. "Let's get inside. Remember, we're newly married, our documents are still in processing. When they ask for ID, and they will, we're going to be out of luck. So, we need to find out as much information as we can before we get to that point."

"I remember." He stepped out of the car.

"Deep breaths, Walt." Samantha followed behind him towards the door of the building. It didn't have much signage, and the parking lot was empty aside from two cars, which she guessed belonged to employees.

"Don't worry, Samantha, this is going to be easy." Walt held the door open for her.

As she stepped inside she glanced at him. Walt was usually the one who was anxious, but somehow their roles had switched. She felt emboldened by his confidence, and headed straight for the front counter. A woman behind it looked up, narrowed her eyes, then offered a smile.

"Welcome, how can I help you today?"

"My husband and I would like to speak to someone about making some investments, please." She smiled in return.

"Oh, okay." She stared at her for a moment, then reached under the desk. With a subtle flap of the paper she placed a form on the counter between them. "Just fill this out and someone will be right with you."

"Thank you." She took the paper and walked over to a small sitting area. Walt joined her on a small, leather couch.

"Do you need a pen, sweetie?" Walt plucked one from his jacket pocket and handed it over to her.

"Thanks." Samantha flashed him a smile then began to fill out the paperwork.

Walt kept his eye on the counter, and the office that was set off to the side of the main lobby. As he expected, a man in a suit stepped out of it, stared at them, then walked up to the counter. He spoke quietly with the woman who had helped them. Then he looked over at them again. As he approached, Walt nudged Samantha lightly with his elbow.

She glanced up in time to see the man stop in front of her.

"Hi there." She kept her voice steady. "We're interested in investing in some properties."

"I'm so glad to hear that. Let me just get your application started." He reached for the paper in her hand.

"Oh, I haven't finished filling it out yet."

"That's all right, we can fill it in as we go." He gestured to the office. "Would you both join me?"

"Sure." Walt stood up, then offered Samantha his hand. She smiled as she accepted it and stood up as well.

After introductions, they settled in his office. Dave Smith seemed like a very important person at the business. A gold nameplate stretched across his desk. The office walls were decorated with fine art. The tall fern in the corner had long, healthy, green leaves.

"Let's just get you started here. What made you choose our company?" He began to tap on the keyboard positioned in front of his computer.

"We heard some good reviews." Samantha nodded.

"Don't be bashful, sweetheart. My wife here, she likes supporting local businesses. She insists we shop at mom and pop stores, and so on. We have been wanting to invest in property for a while and when she discovered your little company here, she insisted we check it out."

"So, no one sent you?" His eyes narrowed slightly.

"No." Samantha blushed. "He's right. But I'm so happy to support your fine business."

"Do you have many local customers?" Walt asked.

"We have a very select clientele." Dave typed a few more things on the keyboard. "We do have a high investment requirement."

"Money is not an issue." Walt sat back in his chair and tried not to think of how many greasy hands had slid across its arms. "Although, it would be nice if I didn't have to declare all of it, if you know what I mean."

"I'm afraid I don't." Dave's expression grew

stern. "I think perhaps this is not the right investment business for you."

"Oh dear, you shouldn't have mentioned that, honey. Listen, we can pay extra." Samantha handed the piece of paper to Dave. "Just name the amount."

"I'm afraid I'm going to have to ask you to leave." He set the paper down on his desk, then stood up.

"Well, all right, we know when we're not wanted." Walt stood up and offered his hand to Samantha. "It's your loss, of course. If you change your mind, feel free to contact me." Walt gazed at him a moment longer, then led the way out of the office.

"We didn't find anything out." Samantha sighed as she pushed the front door of the building open.

"Yes, we did," Walt muttered the words as he guided her out through the door with one hand placed on the center of her back. "It's not a real business."

"It sure looks like one." Samantha glanced over her shoulder, then looked back at him. "What do you mean it's not real?"

"There were no smudges on the counter, or the desk. The floors were spotless. The paperwork on the shelves hasn't been touched in some time, long enough for a thick layer of dust to form on the edges. The only wear in the carpet was from the office to the front door. They don't have regular customers, if they have any customers at all, I'd be shocked."

"So, it's a front?"

"I believe so."

"But for what?" She started the car.

"I'm not sure just yet. But my suspicions are growing."

"And they are?" She glanced over at him before backing the car out of the parking spot.

"I'll let you know when I am certain."

"Walt, this isn't the time to hold anything back. We need to figure out what is going on in there."

"We suspect it's a front. Since it's a property investment business, we can be fairly certain that the crime has to do with money. It could be funneling money internationally, or it could be laundering money for local criminals. My best guess would be that it's laundering money, but that is only a guess."

"Oh, the dirty money the cops in those pictures were passing? That makes sense. They'd have to get it clean somehow. That makes a lot of sense."

"Yes, it does. But that doesn't make it the truth. I'm going to look into the investment business more and see if I can find any evidence of it trafficking money or laundering. If I can, then we'll know what we're dealing with. But until then we shouldn't assume that we've figured it out. Things may be far different than they appear."

"That's true." Samantha sighed as she headed back towards Sage Gardens. "I just hope that whatever they are up to, it's going to lead us to some answers about what happened to Colin."

~

$\mathcal{E}$ddy slid some money into a crisp white envelope, then sealed it. It was far more than he should spend, he knew that, but he didn't want his only lead disappearing. He sent a text to the number that Orin gave him. He knew that he may be giving money to Colin's murderer, but it was worth the risk to get information out of him.

I have cash for you.

An instant later his phone lit up with a text in return that included instructions of where to meet. Eddy slid the envelope into his pocket and headed out the door. His mind was focused on exactly what Orin might be willing to tell him. After speaking with Detective Brunner he felt more confident that he wasn't about to be arrested for Colin's murder, but who else would get the information he'd given to Brunner? Handing over the flash drive had been a big move that he hoped he wouldn't regret. By chain of command, Brunner should hand it over to higher-ups. Would he be wise enough not to?

Eddy pulled into the parking lot that surrounded an abandoned restaurant. The boards on its windows were covered in graffiti, and some hung on by only a few nails. There wasn't another vehicle in sight.

He stepped out of his car and leaned back against it. From this position he could see most of the parking lot and the building. He didn't want to be faced with any surprises.

A few minutes later he saw a figure approach from behind the building. He wore a hooded sweatshirt, with the hood pulled down low over his face. Eddy guessed it was Orin, but he couldn't be certain. The closer the figure came, the more alert his protective instincts became. He wished that he'd brought along something to protect himself, maybe back-up.

"Orin?" Eddy's tone was sharp.

"Yeah, it's me." He pulled the hood back enough

to reveal his face, though it was still shadowed by the hem of the material. "You have the money?"

"I do. But first, I need to know who your main target was. The flash drive didn't reveal it."

"Look, I'm not playing games with you. I'm a dead man if I don't get out of town. I don't owe you any information. Colin convinced me that this could be done, I warned him that it couldn't. Now he's dead, and that's not my fault. I need to move on with my life while I still have one."

"Just tell me who it was." Eddy peered through the shadows at the man's face. "Tell me, and I will take over from here."

"You?" He burst into laughter. "Are you kidding me? You're not even a cop anymore. What do you think you're going to do?"

"I don't have to be a cop to know when something is wrong, Orin. You put yourself on the line this long, why not just tell me the truth so that I can dig further into this?"

"You think I did this out of the goodness of my heart?" He shook his head. "I did this to get out of ten years in lock-up. Colin can't hold that over my head anymore. I don't need to be involved. Give me the money, or I'll just take it from you, those are your choices."

"All right, all right." Eddy cleared his throat. Maybe Orin was right, he was too old to handle things, because his heart started to race in response to the threat. However, as he reached in his pocket for the envelope, a calm washed over him. "First you tell me who killed Colin."

"How am I supposed to know?" He frowned.

"I know that you know." Eddy took a step towards him. "I'm the only one that's going to get you out of town, Orin. What you don't know, is that I have a friend waiting to receive a text from me. If that friend receives my text, then all will be fine. But if that friend doesn't, then the cops will be given your name, location, and evidence that will prove you are the one responsible for Colin's death."

"What proof? I didn't do it! You can't have any proof. You're bluffing, and it's not going to work."

"Am I?" Eddy shrugged. "Are you really ready to risk going down for murder?" He watched the man closely, as he still suspected that Orin might have been the one that killed Colin. If he was, he wasn't showing any signs of guilt.

"All right, fine! You cops are all the same." He curled his lip with disgust. "I don't know who offed the guy, but I do know that Colin was nervous."

"Nervous about the investigation?"

"No, nervous about some guy that got let out of prison. Colin put him behind bars, but the charges were dropped, and the guy was set loose. Apparently, he had been threatening Colin. Colin was worried he might want revenge. That's all I know." He held out his hand. "Money."

"What is the guy's name?" Eddy tapped the envelope against his palm.

"Peter Havershed." He snatched the envelope from Eddy's hand and shook his head. "I guess he got him in the end."

"Maybe. Or maybe you were just tired of being Colin's informant and decided the best way to get out of it was to kill him and blow town."

"I may be a lot of things, in fact, I am." Orin cocked his head to the side and shrugged. "But I'm not a killer. With Colin dead, my life is on the line. Either I'm going to get locked up, or whoever took care of Colin is going to be after me next. Then you."

"Maybe. Any idea where you'll go?"

"Somewhere you'll never find me." He turned and walked away.

Eddy wondered if he'd just given Colin's murderer a way to get out of town. Of course, Orin would say he wasn't a killer, but that didn't mean he wasn't. Still, he doubted that Orin would put himself at so much risk just to get rid of Colin.

As Eddy settled back into the car, he dialed the number of someone he knew from his days on the force, Sandra. She still worked in records at the police department. After a few rings she answered.

"Hi Sandra, I need a favor."

"Eddy, Detective Brunner has warned me that you would be calling."

"He has?"

"Yes, he told me specifically I am not to give you any information regarding the investigation."

"Well, that's fine, because I need information about someone else entirely. A man named Peter Havershed."

"Sure, no problem."

Eddy smiled. Sandra would give him any information he asked for, no matter who told her not to. They'd been friends for a very long time, and they'd lost track of who owed what to who.

"He has a long history of stealing and violence. He was held for robbery and assault. He didn't get bail, but the witness backed out at the last minute and the victim didn't turn up to the trial to give evidence, so without the evidence the charges were dropped. The suspicion was that someone got to them. Peter was released two weeks ago."

"Crazy. They let a criminal run loose?"

"Seems that way. It wouldn't be the first time would it?"

"No, it wouldn't." He frowned. "Thanks for your help, Sandra."

"Be careful, Eddy. Brunner seems nervous about this one."

"I will be, thanks again."

He hung up the phone, then stared out through the windshield. Colin put a man behind bars, and he was set free recently. Could Peter have graduated from assault to murder? Had Peter hunted Colin down and taken his revenge? But if that was the case, where was Peter now?

CHAPTER 13

$\mathcal{A}$s soon as Samantha returned to her villa, she placed a call summoning her friends together for dinner. Walt settled at her computer and began to investigate Sunny River Property Investments.

"Now that I know they are most likely dealing in illegal activity, I may be able to find out more information. This explains why they have such little information on the internet."

"Good, Jo and Eddy are on their way." She sat down at the table with him. "Walt, I have to say I'm pretty impressed. I never would have noticed all of the things you did at their office. I really thought we'd wasted our time there."

"You think being married to me is a waste of time?" He winked at her.

"Jokes now, too?" Samantha grinned. "I think you're coming out of your shell, Walt."

"Hmm, maybe I should be more careful." He brushed his fingertips along his shoulder. "Wouldn't want to be too noticeable."

"There's nothing wrong with being noticeable."

"Actually, statistics show that there is a much larger risk of being targeted for numerous crimes if you have a more visible presence." He glanced up from the computer. "I'll stay in my shell thank you."

"I'll make us some tea." Samantha patted his shoulder as she walked past him and into the kitchen.

A few minutes later a knock on the door signaled Jo's arrival. When Samantha opened the door, she noticed the paleness of Jo's skin.

"Are you okay?"

"Of course, I am." She smiled. "Is Eddy here, yet?"

"Not yet. He should be here soon, though."

"I'm here now." Eddy stepped through the door. He glanced around at his friends, then pulled off his fedora. "It seems we have a situation."

"A situation?" Samantha looked into his eyes.

"This man." Eddy held up his phone with a picture of Peter Havershed on the display. "He was recently released from prison, he was being held on suspicion of robbery and assault. He was released because the victim and witness backed out of testifying and there wasn't enough against him, even though Colin both arrested and testified against him. It's very possible that he is the killer."

"Pete?" Samantha's eyes widened.

"You know him?" Jo stepped up beside her with narrowed eyes.

"Yes, well no, I've met him." Samantha looked up at Eddy. "He was the doorman at the party. He sat with me and had a drink while you were outside."

"You had a drink with him?" Eddy's eyes widened. "Samantha, he is a violent criminal."

"I had no idea." She stared at him. "He spilled his drink on me, and then my drink, we just had a casual conversation. He gave me his card." She walked over to her purse and dug through it until she came up with the business card he'd handed her. "Honestly, I never even looked at it." She handed it over to Eddy.

"Just his name and a phone number. How strange." He flipped the card over, then looked back at Samantha. "I hate the thought that you were alone with someone like this."

"Now, wait a minute." Jo frowned. "It's a big leap to go from assault to murder. If he was released, isn't it possible that he was innocent?"

"It's possible. But it seems like the witness was scared off," Eddy said.

"Even if he was innocent of that crime, that doesn't mean he's innocent of Colin's murder." Walt tapped a fingertip on the table. "One does not cancel out the other."

"Well, I don't think that Peter was actually innocent. I think the victim and witness were intimidated. Which means there's a criminal on the loose. A criminal that apparently had it in for Colin. I can't help but wonder if he picked you out to sit with for a reason, Sam." He looked into her eyes.

"You mean other than seeing a desirable woman alone?" She raised an eyebrow.

"Yes, I do mean that." He rested his hands on the table as he gazed at her and blushed slightly. "You are a beautiful woman, Sam, there is no question about that. But Peter was there for a reason, and I believe he sat down with you for a reason as well."

"It seems pretty obvious that he was there to

target Colin." Jo sat down at the table beside Samantha.

"It seems like a stretch. He would have to get the job there, and know Colin was going to be at the party. Wouldn't Colin have recognized him at the door and done something? And he didn't have the time to commit the murder, he was with me until I went out to check on Eddy. Doesn't that eliminate him as a suspect?"

"Not exactly." Eddy frowned. "I waited ten minutes after Colin left to go outside to meet him. Then it was still a few minutes more before Peter sat down with you, right Sam?"

"Right." She nodded. "He would have had time to go in the kitchen and kill Colin. It doesn't take very long to do something like that. But he didn't have any evidence on his clothes."

"Was he still wearing his uniform?" Eddy asked.

"No." Samantha's eyes widened. "No, he said his shift was over, and he was allowed to have some cake and champagne."

"So, he could have killed Colin, then changed out of his uniform, and sat down with you so that he would have an alibi." Eddy shook his head. "That sounds like a pretty good plan to me."

"Yes, I have to admit, you're right." Samantha

frowned. "But what does that say about my instincts?"

"At that time we had no reason to even suspect that anything happened to Colin. You were relaxed." Eddy looked over at Jo. "Are you ready to fill us in on what's going on with you?"

"What?" She blinked, then stared back at him.

"He's right." Samantha tipped her head to the side so that she could look at her. "I noticed it, too."

"She'll tell us when she's ready," Walt said. "Samantha and I paid a visit to the property investment company associated with the symbols written on the money, and I am fairly certain that it is a front for a criminal enterprise. After doing a bit more digging I've identified at least three known felons that have a connection to the company."

"Interesting." Eddy nodded. "So that's why Colin drew the symbols on the bill. He was trying to send a message, just in case. That's why he left me the note with the money." He sighed. "He knew that there was a chance he wouldn't be alive much longer."

"With good reason." Jo stared down at the table.

"What's that?" Eddy's attention shifted to her. "Ready to share?"

"Look, before I do, I want all of you to understand that I am aware I made a mistake. I don't want to hear any lectures. Got it?" She gazed at Eddy, then looked pointedly at Walt. "Not from either of you."

"No lectures." Walt held up his hands.

"What did you do?" Eddy squinted at her.

Jo shifted uncomfortably in her chair as all eyes turned on her. She never enjoyed such focused attention.

"I thought I'd take a look at Hank a little closer. See what hidden secrets he had at home." She shrugged. "I wanted to get an idea of what we were really dealing with."

"You broke into his house?" Eddy's voice raised a notch. "Have you lost your mind?"

"No lectures." She quirked a brow.

"Jo." Walt sighed as he stared at her. "You know that—"

"Enough." Samantha held up a hand in each of their directions. "Let her speak. What happened, Jo?"

"I got caught." She grimaced. "It's the first time in a very long time that has happened to me. He must have had some kind of remote video link to the house. I was in his office, and I found a drawer full of cash." She held up her phone and displayed the pictures she'd taken.

"Full of cash?" Walt looked into her eyes. "Can you be more specific on the amount?"

"Maybe one hundred thousand, maybe a lot more. I didn't have time to count it."

"Then what happened?" Samantha stared at her.

"Somehow Hank knew I was there. He came in the house, and I had no choice but to meet him face-to-face. I thought for sure he was going to kill me or have me arrested, but instead he quizzed me about what I'd seen, and then let me leave."

"He just let you walk out?" Eddy's mouth dropped open in disbelief. "Hank Greer?"

"Yes. I know, it was strange. But he wasn't shy about threatening me. He's a very intimidating man."

"Yes, he is." Eddy frowned. "I promised no lectures, Jo, but I am going to tell you how relieved I am that you are okay. Things could have easily turned out far differently."

"I know." Jo gazed at the table. "Trust me, I know."

She looked up as Walt placed his hand on the curve of her shoulder.

"I'm sorry that happened, Jo. It must have left

you shaken."

"Yes, it did." She shook her head. "But we need to stay focused."

"Okay, wait just a minute." Samantha raised her hand into the air and looked directly at Jo. "I have something to say."

"What?" Jo stared at her.

"They promised no lectures, I didn't. Jo, what were you thinking?"

"Samantha, I—"

"You just thought it would be perfectly acceptable for you to run off on your own, when you have three capable friends who could have accompanied you? You thought you'd put your life at risk and tempt a madman without consulting any of us?"

"Sam." Eddy put a hand on her shoulder. "Take a breath, dear, I think Jo has been through enough."

"You're wrong." She brushed his hand away. "Jo, you have to promise me that you won't do anything like that again. I mean it. What if something terrible had happened?"

"Okay, okay." Jo took her hand, and held it in a snug grasp. "I promise."

"Thank you." Samantha sighed with relief. "What about the flash drive? Don't you think we should give it to Detective Brunner? If we don't, we're interfering with the investigation, and that could come back on us." She looked over at Eddy.

"I already turned it in. Detective Brunner knows everything that we do now. Well, everything but what we recently found out. I went out on a limb and trusted Brunner, now it's up to him to prove whether he's trustworthy or not. He's trusted me before, and I decided it was best to extend him the same courtesy."

"Risky." Jo pursed her lips.

"I think you did the right thing." Samantha nodded. "You didn't really have any other choice."

"I guess soon we will find out whether he is involved in all of this." Walt folded his hands on the table.

"Yes, we will. Until then, we need to be very careful. At this point we have a few suspects, and no real direction to follow. Orin should be headed out of town, and Hank could easily flee as well. Peter will have a harder time disappearing, especially since he is using his real name."

"I think we have two other suspects as well." Samantha glanced around at the others. "Hank Greer's son, Mitch and his friend, Riley. Remember the way they spoke to Colin at the party? Colin seemed a bit bothered by whatever they said."

"You're right." Eddy nodded. "We can't rule them out, they might be involved in this. Maybe they were trying to keep Colin off Hank's back."

"We have our work cut out for us." Samantha sighed.

"I can tell you this much, if Hank was so quick to let me go, it's because he had a lot to hide. The money in that drawer wasn't there for no reason. He doesn't know that I found it, but if he figures it out, I'll be on his hit list." Jo crossed her arms, with a hint of blush in her cheeks.

"We all will be." Eddy frowned. "Walt and I will go speak with Mitch tomorrow morning to see if we can find out anything more about his father. None of us should go anywhere near Hank Greer, understood?" He looked between Samantha and Jo.

"Understood." Jo nodded.

"Yes." Samantha frowned. "But I don't think we should overlook Pete. I'm going to see if I can track him down."

"If you do, let Detective Brunner know where you've found him, and let him handle it." Eddy tapped his knuckles on the table. "This is dangerous business, and I don't want anyone getting hurt."

They all nodded.

CHAPTER 14

*O*n his way home, Eddy's mind was clouded with concern. He knew that the deeper they dug into the crime, the more at risk they would all become.

Eddy glanced at his cell phone as it rang on the seat beside him. He slowed the car and pulled off to the side of the road. He wasn't one for talking and driving. Samantha had tried to get him to use a handsfree device, but he found the whole process too stressful.

When he noticed the name on the caller ID his body grew tense. Why would Detective Brunner be calling him? Did he get wind of the fact that Eddy's friends in the department had given him information, or had he come across some evidence that would implicate him? There was only one way to find out.

Eddy answered the phone with a slight strain in his voice.

"Hello, Detective."

"Eddy, I'm glad you answered. I wanted to update you on some information I've come across."

"Oh?" Eddy knew he had some information to share with the detective as well.

"The money that you turned in, it's been found to be dirty. It's been linked to an armed robbery."

"Really?" Eddy's heart skipped a beat.

"Yes, so if you were planning to spend any of it, you should keep in mind that you're going to get caught."

"I turned it in."

"I know, just trying to share a bit of humor with you. As I was saying, since the money is dirty, and it was originally in Colin's possession, according to you, we are now looking into whether Colin may have been involved in criminal activities, possibly even a money laundering operation that could have led to his murder. Do you know anything about that?"

"You're back to thinking I'm part of some kind of criminal conspiracy?"

"I'm back to thinking that you know a lot more about this crime than you're letting on. So, did you know anything about the dirty money?"

"No, not until I found it. I thought maybe he left it for me deliberately." Eddy wanted the detective to believe that he left it for him without telling him about the note. He didn't think the detective would appreciate that he had been keeping it from him.

"For you?"

"Yes, I thought maybe he left it for me to give me an idea of what was happening."

"And, what do you know about it?"

"Listen, I don't know anything about the dirty money. But you may want to look into Sunny River Property Investments. I have reason to suspect that it is involved somehow."

"Why?"

"Just a hunch." Eddy shrugged. "That's all I know."

"All right, I'll do that."

"What about Peter Havershed?"

"We are aware of his presence at the party, however we haven't been able to locate him just yet. We're actively looking. I suppose you figured that out on your own?"

"With a little help." He cleared his throat. "Listen, Detective, we can be on the same team here."

"No, actually we can't. Because you're giving me information piece by piece instead of telling me the whole story. Eddy, you know I admire you, and your career in the force, but I can't simply let you run wild on this case. You are personally involved, and you are retired."

"So I keep hearing. Fine, you do what you need to do, and I'll do what I need to do. Thanks, Detective." He hung up the phone. Then he drove the short distance to his villa and parked in the driveway.

As Eddy walked up to the door, he noticed something was wrong right away. The door was open about an inch. He never left his door unlocked, let alone open. He walked the perimeter of the villa, and peeked in the windows. He didn't see any sign of anyone inside, but he did notice that all of his belongings were strewn across the floor. When he reached the front door again, he stepped carefully inside.

Glass was shattered from picture frames knocked to the ground. All of the drawers in his tables had been emptied out. In the kitchen, all of the drawers and cabinets had been emptied. He'd never seen such a mess, and as his heart pounded against his chest, he realized that whoever had been in his villa might not have found what they were looking for.

Eddy's hands shook with anger as he began to clean up the scattered boxes of food and dishes. In the back of his mind he knew that he should report this to Brunner, so that they could check for DNA and fingerprints. But he doubted there would be any left behind. Was the person looking for the flash drive? If they were they would be back to look for it again, and if Eddy was there the next time, things might get more than messy. Was it Orin that had rummaged through his villa? Maybe he was looking for more money? Was it Peter, in search of any evidence against him? Or was it Hank Greer himself? Maybe after Jo broke into his place he decided to find out more about her and he linked them all together. The thought made him shudder. He grabbed his phone and placed a call to Samantha. When she answered he spoke breathlessly.

"Samantha, are you okay?"

"Sure, I'm fine, but you don't sound okay. What's wrong?"

"Lock your door!"

"It is locked."

"Double check."

"Eddy, what is this about?" She sighed into the phone.

"Just keep your doors locked, and check on Jo and Walt too, please." Eddy hung up the phone, then returned to cleaning up what he could. A few minutes later there was a sharp knock at the door. He jumped at the sound. "Who is it?" He braced himself for the possibility that whoever had ransacked his villa had returned.

"It's me, Eddy." Samantha pushed the door open, then gasped when she saw the disaster beyond it. "What happened here?"

"Sam, I didn't ask you to come."

"The tone of your voice did." She looked up at him. "Did someone break in?"

"Yes, of course."

"Did you call the police?"

"They might be the ones who did this." He narrowed his eyes. "I'm not telling them about this."

"I'll help you clean up." She waded her way through the scattered belongings into the kitchen and retrieved a broom and dustpan. They worked quietly together to get the villa back into shape.

"At least they didn't hurt my chair." Eddy patted the top of his favorite recliner.

"Oh yes, that's good at least." Samantha scrunched up her nose as a small dust cloud drifted off the chair. "You can't stay here tonight. You can stay at my place. If you're serious about not telling Brunner, then I at least need to know that you're safe."

"Fine. That's probably a good idea. I'll let Walt and Jo know to stick together tonight as well. I'm concerned that whoever broke in here could target all of us."

"Do you think it was Greer?"

"It could have been him, or Orin, or Peter, or even Greer's son. There's no way to know for sure."

"You must be exhausted. Let's go, Eddy. There's nothing more we can do here tonight."

"All right." Eddy nodded. "I'll just grab some things."

After Eddy collected a few essentials, he followed Samantha out the door. He made sure his door was locked.

*E*arly the next morning Samantha's phone began to ring. She was jolted fully awake by the name that displayed on her phone. Detective Brunner.

"Hello?"

"Samantha, we still need to have our interview. Can you come in now?"

"I'll need at least a half hour to get ready. I was sleeping." She wiped her eyes then peered at the time on the clock on her bedside table. "It's barely seven."

"I apologize, we've had some developments in the case and I need you to answer some questions for me. The sooner, the better. Is that possible?"

"Yes, of course. Anything I can do to help." She bit into her bottom lip as she recalled the destruction in Eddy's apartment the night before. After she hung up with the detective she headed into the kitchen to make some coffee. No matter what, she had to have it before she could start her day.

"Was that Brunner?" Eddy's sleep-logged voice made her jump. She glanced over to see him on the couch, still tangled up in the blanket she'd given him the night before.

"Yes, he wants me to come in for an interview. I need to be there as soon as I can."

"It's early." Eddy managed to fight off the blanket and got to his feet. "He must be on to something."

"He said he had questions he needed to ask me."

"You didn't tell him about the break-in, did you?" He watched as she poured them both a cup of coffee.

"No, I didn't. But maybe we should. Brunner seems to be trustworthy."

"And if he's not? Or if he passes the information to the wrong person? The more the killer knows about us, the more danger we are in. I agree with you, Sam, the right thing to do is to tell Brunner, unfortunately we're not in the best of circumstances. I would never ask you to lie for me, Sam. If you feel it's best to tell Brunner the truth, then I will accept and respect that. I'm just asking you to think about it."

"I will." She frowned, then took a sip of her coffee. It was difficult to decide what to do. She suspected from the images and videos on the flash drive that there were a few police officers involved in this crime in some way, and yet her instincts told her she could trust Brunner. After she finished her coffee, she dressed. "I'll be back as quickly as I can." Samantha grabbed her purse.

"Walt and I are going to go speak with Mitch. Hopefully we can find out something from him. Good luck with Detective Brunner."

"Be careful." Samantha gave him a quick hug, then headed out the door. As she drove towards the police station her mind swirled with all of the questions that Brunner might want to ask her. When she arrived, the parking lot was fairly empty. Inside, she found Detective Brunner at the front desk. He led her back to his office, then closed the door.

"Samantha, thank you for coming in so quickly. We have a lot of ground to cover."

"Of course." She sat down across from him. "Anything you need."

"I understand you had a conversation with Peter Havershed at the party?"

"Yes, I did. It was brief."

"Not so brief that you aren't serving as his alibi." He smiled as he looked into her eyes. "Was he with you the entire time? He didn't leave to use the bathroom, or anything like that?"

"He only left the table to get us both drinks, but I saw him go to the bar. So no, he never left my sight." She frowned. "That doesn't mean he's not the killer, though. There was still time for him to commit the crime."

"Yes, I know there was." He sighed. "But it does tighten the time frame and make him a less likely suspect. What I need to know from you is if you noticed anything off about him. Any stains on his clothes?"

"Well, he spilled my drink, and then his drink. Some of it did get on to his shirt. But, I didn't notice anything before that."

"Okay." He made a note, then looked back up at her. "And how did he seem to you? Relaxed? Anxious?"

"He said he was nervous about joining me, and that's why he spilled the drink. But in general he was normal." She sighed. "Honestly, he was warm, friendly, I'd say a little flirtatious. He didn't strike me as a criminal, that's for sure."

"I'd guess not." He leaned back in his chair. "So, you two just chatted?"

"He gave me his card. He wanted to pay for the dry cleaning of my dress, but I told him not to worry about it."

"That was nice of you."

"I thought I was talking to a nice person. I had no idea about his past."

"Of course, you didn't. There was no way that

you could have known."

"I don't understand how Colin didn't see him when he entered the lobby."

"Oh, good question." The detective nodded. "Apparently, Peter had just returned from his break and you and Eddy were the first people he opened the door for after his break. From what I've managed to ascertain, Colin arrived about ten minutes before you and Eddy so they would have missed each other."

"Okay." Samantha nodded.

"What about anyone else at the party? Did anyone else pay particular attention to Colin?"

"The only other people I saw speak to him were Hank Greer's son, Mitch and his friend, Riley. Mitch whispered something to Colin which he seemed to get upset about."

"Okay, that's something to look into. Eddy seems to be very hesitant with giving me information, which isn't like him at all."

"Colin's murder made him nervous. It made us all nervous."

"You suspect me as well?" He smiled some. "I guess I shouldn't be surprised. I've read some of your articles and you always go straight for the truth."

"It's the most important thing to me."

"So, you should understand why it's what I need the most right now." He rested his chin on his fingertips and studied her. "What's really going on with Eddy?"

"He lost his friend." Samantha gritted her teeth as the urge to reveal information about the break-in welled up within her. "Of course, he's going to be upset and even acting a little strangely."

"Of course." Detective Brunner nodded. "But I want you to know, Samantha, if there's ever anything that you want to talk to me about, I'll be here. All right?"

"Yes, I understand." She smiled politely. "Thank you, Detective."

He stood up and walked her to the door.

"Samantha, I know that after seeing what was on that flash drive, you probably have a lot of questions about who can be trusted. I just want you to know that I can be."

"I'll keep that in mind." Samantha nodded as she stepped through the door, but a part of her couldn't help noticing that he seemed determined to convince her. Maybe a little too determined.

CHAPTER 15

The tension in the furniture factory was palpable. Eddy glanced through the open doors from the lobby at the workers who were all in action, whether it was on the phone, handling machinery, or arguing with each other.

"Can I see Mr. Greer?" He asked the receptionist who had just hung up the phone.

"He's in the back. Down that hall, first door." She rolled her eyes.

"Thanks." Eddy had the sense that Mitch was not well-liked.

"Ugh, when was the last time they cleaned these floors?" Walt tore his shoe out of a sticky spot, as his face grew pale. "I will get the mop myself if they'll let me."

"Try to relax, Walt, we're not here for that. Remember? We can't get distracted."

"Yes, you're right." He gritted his teeth. "But really, it's not that hard to clean up spills."

Eddy pushed the door open to a sectioned off area of the factory. Inside were a few small desks, and quite a bit of space. The room was spotless, warmer than the rest of the factory, and even smelled quite a bit better. Seated at two of the desks towards the back of the room were Riley and Mitch. They both looked up as Eddy and Walt approached.

"Hey Eddy!" Riley smiled. "What are you doing here, old man?"

"Checking on you two." Eddy crossed his arms. "I've heard some rumors about you being involved in something dirty."

Walt tensed as he glanced over at Eddy. He hadn't expected him to come right out and say it.

"Dirty, huh?" Mitch tucked some paperwork into the drawer in his desk.

"You two should really shower more often." Eddy chuckled.

"Oh, he has jokes!" Riley laughed and slapped his hands together. "Trust me, I haven't gotten any complaints. Now, Mitch on the other hand."

"Quiet." Mitch rolled his eyes. "Why are you really here, Eddy?"

"Listen, I've got a bit of a problem." He sat down in a chair near their desks. "Maybe you could help me out with it?"

"Sure." Mitch looked Walt over. "Who's this?"

"A good friend of mine. Take a seat, Walt." Eddy gestured to the chair beside him.

Walt pulled a tissue out of his pocket and wiped it over the seat of the chair, then sat down.

"Okay?" Riley raised an eyebrow. "So, what's going on?"

"Here's the thing. A friend of mine found something. He didn't know what it was at the time. But it turned out to be some very incriminating evidence against some people including a very powerful man that is involved in a criminal enterprise. Now, he wants to know if he should turn that in to the police. But I warned him that he shouldn't get involved. He wouldn't listen to me. I thought maybe we should go to your dad with this, but he's such a tough guy to get in touch with."

"Yeah, he can be. What kind of evidence is it?" Mitch locked eyes with him.

"Some pictures, some videos, you know that kind of thing. Pretty dire stuff. I told him, just drop it down a drain somewhere or toss it in a fire. But he refused, so, here I am."

"Why exactly are you here?" Mitch continued to hold his gaze.

"I thought maybe you could get your dad to see him." Eddy shrugged.

"I don't think he will, without knowing what it's about. He'll need more information. I think you should tell him to get rid of it." Mitch glanced at Riley.

"Maybe we could help you convince him," Riley said.

"Look, my dad won't speak to him without knowing more. If your friend is in as much danger as you claim, he should get rid of the evidence." Mitch shrugged. "That way his name stays out of everything."

"Great advice, I agree, I'll try to convince him." Eddy narrowed his eyes. "I appreciate your time."

"Anytime." Mitch stood up. "Is there anything else I can help you with?"

"No, that's it."

"Actually." Walt smiled as he looked at the two men. "Could either of you explain to me the state of the floor in the entrance? I'd really like to know why it's come to the point it has. Perhaps I could make a donation to provide the janitor with more efficient and effective cleaning supplies?"

"It's that way for a reason. The janitor has had a few days off and the company won't pay for agency staff. The factory workers hate cleaning, they don't think it's part of their job, so it never gets done." Riley chuckled. "The workers would rather stand around out front and smoke."

"Ah, I see. But I noticed this area is very clean. A different cleaning crew?" Walt asked.

"Yes, well sort of." Riley shrugged. "We like to keep it clean and tidy ourselves. So we can have clear minds."

"My sentiments exactly." Walt grinned. "It was a pleasure meeting both of you."

As they left the factory, Eddy glanced over at Walt.

"What was all that about?"

"I was just curious. It seems that they like to do things themselves. Maybe for the sake of privacy. I think they might be hiding something."

"I agree. I think they're trying to protect Hank."

"Are you sure?" Walt stared at him. "How can you be?"

"I'm not sure. But Mitch suggested my friend get rid of the evidence. I think he just may suspect it is evidence against his father. I think he is trying to make sure that it never comes to light. The fact that he encouraged that meant that he didn't want that evidence to be revealed. Of course, I can't be sure about that, but my instincts tell me those two are up to something, and I'm going to find out exactly what it is."

~

Samantha pushed open the door to her villa and found Eddy, Walt, and Jo, sitting at her table with lunch already prepared for all of them.

"Hi." She smiled as she pulled the purse off her shoulder. "Thanks for the grub." She grabbed one of the sandwiches and sat down. "I'm starving."

"How did the meeting go?" Eddy pushed a can of soda towards her.

"Great." She caught it. "Brunner says we should trust him. I think we should, too. But I didn't tell him about the break-in."

"Speaking of the break-in, I think we all need to be cautious. If they are after the flash drive and they think Eddy gave it to one of us, then all of our places could be ransacked." Jo glanced around the table.

"Yes, it's possible." Eddy tapped his fingertips on the table. "But I'm not going to wait for that to happen. Walt and I paid a visit to Mitch and Riley today and I think they are trying to protect Hank. I think they might even possibly be involved in these crimes with him. I say we stake out Sunny River tonight, and see who shows up. My best guess if it's anyone it will be Hank Greer."

"You and Samantha could stake out the company, and Walt and I could sit on Hank Greer's place." Jo winced. "Although, we need to make sure he doesn't catch me. That would be a disaster."

"Yes, it would be." Eddy glanced at his watch. "I think it's too big of a risk. We'll stake out Sunny River and you and Walt see if you can find out more information about Hank and Peter. Then you can join us and take over if the night drags on." He frowned as his cell phone buzzed. When he saw the message, his face grew pale. "Well, well, apparently Orin is still in town."

"He is?" Samantha's eyes widened.

"He wants a meeting. I'd better get over there now." Eddy stood up.

"Wait, I want to go with you." Samantha took

the last bite of her sandwich then stood up to join him.

"Sam, maybe that's not such a good idea."

"Eddy, if we're going to be a team, that means we all need to have an idea of what we're dealing with. Orin could be the killer just as easily as Hank. Apparently, the least likely suspect is Pete, but I certainly wouldn't rule him out. I just want to look into Orin's eyes and get a feel for him. All right?" She smiled, a stony expression coated in the sweetness of her curved lips. She was not about to budge.

"All right, fine."

"I'll see what Jo and I can trace about Pete's recent activities, too." Walt nodded. "He has to be spending money somewhere."

"Great idea." Samantha smiled, then followed Eddy out the door.

"You have to let me take the lead on this, okay?" Eddy glanced over his shoulder at her as they headed for the driveway. "Orin won't like another person being there and I'm not sure how he will respond to it."

"If Jo can handle Hank, then I can handle Orin."

"Samantha." He looked into her eyes. "You're a tough lady, I'll give you that, but you're not Jo."

"What is that supposed to mean?" She raised an eyebrow.

"It means that you've never lived as a criminal. Have you?"

"No, I guess I haven't. But I still think I can handle it."

"We're about to find out." Eddy popped open the passenger side door for her, then rounded the car to the driver's side.

As they pulled out of the driveway a ripple of uncertainty caused Samantha to shiver. She'd been in some difficult circumstances, but perhaps she'd boasted a bit too much about how much she could handle.

The short drive ended in the parking lot of a rundown bar. She again questioned her ability to face what was inside. However, with Eddy beside her, her confidence spiked.

He glanced over at her, then stepped out of the car. She waited until he was on her side of the car before she stepped out as well. He gazed at her a moment longer.

"Are you sure about this? I don't know what exactly we're walking into."

"Yes, I'm sure." Samantha smiled and slid her arm through his. "Let's go find out."

Eddy's lips tensed as if he might say more, but instead he nodded, and headed to the door. When he opened it, there was silence and the bar was dark.

"Samantha, wait here." Eddy gave her a look that left no room for argument. He took a few steps into the bar, then looked back over his shoulder. "Call Brunner, now. Tell him to get over here."

"All right, I will. What's happened?" Samantha tried to look past Eddy, but couldn't see anything.

Samantha gave Brunner the address of the bar. For once he didn't ask multiple questions, instead he said he would be there in minutes.

"Eddy?" Samantha took a small step inside the bar. "Detective Brunner is on his way, now can you tell me what's happened?"

"It's Orin." He looked back at Samantha. "He's dead, he's been stabbed. I'm going to check in the back to make sure Rex isn't here."

"Be careful, Eddy!"

"I will be. Stay right here." Eddy looked hard into her eyes. "I mean it."

"I will."

Samantha wrung her hands as she looked at the body on the floor. It made her nervous to consider that the same person who had killed Colin, had likely killed Orin, which meant that he had no problem with committing multiple murders. "Eddy?"

"I'm here, there's no one back here."

Detective Brunner announced his presence as he burst through the door.

Samantha jumped and gave a short scream.

"It's okay, it's just me." Brunner lowered his weapon. "Where's Eddy?"

"Here." Eddy stepped out of the back. "There's no one else here."

"Who is this?" Brunner gazed down at the body.

"Orin Banks." Eddy sighed and filled him in on everything he knew about Orin.

"Wait, are you telling me you didn't turn him in to me?" Brunner's voice wavered with anger.

"I did what I thought was best. I thought I was protecting him, like Colin would want me to." Eddy's cheeks reddened.

"Clear out of here." Brunner looked from Eddy, to Samantha. "Both of you. I'm going to need to get a team in here." He sighed as he looked back at Eddy. "You do realize that the two of you have now been at the scene of two homicides."

"We just walked in, and Orin was there." Samantha frowned. "You have to believe us."

"I do." He looked into Eddy's eyes, then shook his head. "Anything else you want to tell me?"

"I've told you everything." Eddy slid his hands into his pockets.

"I wish I could believe that." The detective turned his attention back to the body.

Samantha nudged Eddy with her elbow.

He frowned.

She nudged him again.

"Actually. Someone might have broken into my place last night."

"Might have?" Brunner looked back at Eddy.

"Did." Eddy cleared his throat. "They were looking for something. Probably the flash drive that I gave you."

"I'll send a team over to check out the place." Brunner reached for his phone.

"Don't bother I already cleaned it up. There was nothing to find."

"Eddy, you make it really hard for me to work with you." He pursed his lips. "Tomorrow I'm going to send someone out to question your neighbors and see if anyone saw who broke in."

"Fine." Eddy nodded. "Let's go, Samantha."

As they headed back to the car, Samantha's stomach churned.

"Now we know that Orin probably didn't do it. Which only leaves Pete, and Hank. What if we're wrong and it's someone we haven't even considered?"

"That's always a possibility." Eddy nodded. "Detective Brunner has the same suspects, so I think we're on the right track. Hopefully, the stakeout tonight at Sunny River will tell us something."

CHAPTER 16

"*H*ave you found anything?" Jo leaned over Walt's shoulder.

"Not since two minutes ago, when you asked me." He glanced up at her. "I am doing the best I can, Jo."

"I know you are, I'm sorry. This whole thing is just making me really nervous. The sooner we can figure out who did this, the calmer I'll feel."

"The calmer we'll all feel." Walt nodded. "But it is hard for me to concentrate when you're so close to me." He raised an eyebrow.

"I know, I know, sorry." She began to pace again.

"That's not much better. Here, why don't you help me look?" He slid his chair over some. "Eddy managed to get me a copy of Peter Havershed's accounts. We're trying to find information on Peter, where he might have been in the past few days. If you were Peter, where would you go? Where would you spend money?"

"That's easy. Nowhere. At least not on a card." Jo shrugged.

"But he wouldn't have a lot of cash. It looks like he's getting some direct deposit income from some source, maybe his job at the hotel. He hasn't made any cash withdrawals from his account. So how is he living?"

"Maybe he's pawning things. Maybe he pawned things from the robbery and is using that to survive." Jo nodded. "And since he's been in this area." She leaned past him and typed in a few quick words. "There. 'Don's Pawn and More'. That's the place he'd go."

"But there are several more pawn shops in the area, how do you know that's where he would go?"

"He's open to fencing stolen items. Most pawn shops have strict rules about what they will accept. Don's philosophy is that if he has a buyer, then he will take it. Don't ask me how I know, just trust me. Let's take a drive over, hmm?"

"A pawn shop?" Walt cringed. "So many dirty, dusty things."

"I know, but you won't have to touch anything." Jo smiled and patted his back.

"Promise?" He followed her to the door.

"Promise." Jo winked at him.

Walt followed her directions to the pawn shop, and he could only assume that she'd been there several times. It was a small place with only a sign in the front window. As they approached it, a man stepped out, glanced at them, then hurried off down the sidewalk.

"Are you sure this is a safe place?" Walt frowned.

"As safe as it can be." Jo held open the door for him so that he wouldn't have to touch the handle. When they stepped inside, a man behind the counter turned to face them.

"Jo?" He stared at her. "Is that really you?"

"Yes." She laughed. "It's me, Don."

"Wow, it's been quite some time."

"I know. I've been a bit busy." She walked up to the counter. Walt hung back by the door, his gaze focused on the shelves full of unsorted items.

"Well, what did you bring me? Something fantastic, I'm sure."

"No, sorry. Only a question." She held up her cell phone with a picture of Peter on display. "Is this one of your customers?"

"Pete? Yeah. Why?" He narrowed his eyes. "Are you working for the cops now?"

"No, nothing like that. Actually, my friend over there." She gestured to Walt, who seemed to be frozen in place, horrified by the chaos on the shelves. "He sold something to Pete, and Pete paid him in counterfeit bills." Jo hoped that would scare him into telling her something.

"Oh yeah?" His cheeks grew red. "You're sure about that?"

"Yes. That's why we're trying to track him down. You didn't take any cash from him did you, for anything?"

"No, he bought something from me using some of his stuff instead of money." Don shrugged.

"Did he tell you where he's staying?" She pursed her lips. "I want to settle things with him."

"I understand that, Jo, but he didn't tell me anything. People don't exactly fill out registration cards when they shop here." He stared at Walt. "Is he okay?"

"He's fine. What did he buy from you?"

"Uh, a couple of knives." Don lowered his voice.

"You know, I'm not supposed to sell those, but this is just between us."

"Right." Her heart dropped. Colin had been stabbed. Was it possible that Peter used a knife he'd bought from the pawn shop. "Did he mention any place he might hang out? Anywhere he enjoyed visiting while he was here?"

"No, nothing. I don't really get into in-depth conversations with customers. Unless they look like you of course." Don smiled as he gazed into her eyes.

"What about video?" Walt finally turned to the counter. "I see you have three cameras in here."

"You do?" Don stared at him. "How did you know that? They're hidden."

"Not well. So, do you have anything on camera that might help us? Maybe his vehicle? Or someone else who was with him?"

"Look, if there was something there that could help, I would tell you. But I wipe the cameras every day. I haven't seen Peter in a few days. There's nothing on there that would help. I'm sorry. But, Jo promise me you're not going to be a stranger, eh?"

"I can assure you, she will be." Walt slipped his arm around hers. "Unless you begin to clean and organize this place properly."

"What?" Don stared after them as they walked out of the shop.

"That was interesting, Walt." She laughed as she reached the car.

"It's the truth. You shouldn't breathe air that dusty, it's not good for you."

"Always looking out for me, Walt, I appreciate that." Jo buckled her seat belt, then frowned. "Too bad we didn't find out anything that could help the investigation. Maybe Pete bought the murder weapon here, but that doesn't get us any closer to him."

"Unfortunately, not. Oh dear." He studied a text on his phone. "It's from Eddy. Orin's been killed. They're on their way to stake out Sunny River."

"Two murders now." Jo shook her head. "This isn't looking good."

~

*E*ddy parked the car in the back of a grocery store parking lot that was adjacent to the property investment company. A short trek over a grassy space was all it would take to get to the company itself. It provided a clear view of the side and rear of the business.

"I have a feeling we're in for a long wait." Samantha stretched her legs, then looked over at Eddy. "How are you holding up?"

"Okay." He frowned. "It's not like I knew Orin well, but it worries me to think that two people I was with were killed in almost as many days. I never should have gotten you, or Walt, or Jo, involved in all of this."

"We're involved because we want to be." She placed her hand on his shoulder and looked into his eyes. "Eddy, if you have a problem, we all have a problem, got it?"

"Thanks, Sam."

"Wait a minute, isn't that Riley?" Samantha sat forward in the car. She kept her gaze focused out through the windshield as a figure walked towards Sunny River Property Investments. With the fading sunlight, it was difficult to get a clear view, but he looked young.

"It could be." Eddy watched as the figure knocked on the side door. A few seconds later, the door swung open, and the figure disappeared inside. "I'm going to take a closer look. You stay here, be my lookout, let me know if anyone else shows up, okay?"

"But—"

"Samantha, I'm serious. I need you to have my back on this. I can't have someone catching me skulking outside the building. Can I trust you to keep a lookout?"

"Yes, of course you can." She was more than a little disappointed to have to stay in the car, but she knew that Eddy was right. She watched him go, until he disappeared into the shadows created by the overhang of the company's roof.

Eddy made his way along the wall of the building until he reached a tall window that allowed a view inside. The lobby was dark, but there was light spilling from a few doors. He could see long shadows cast by more than one person inside one of the rooms. Unfortunately, that was all he could see. He ran quickly past the window to the next portion of the wall. When his cell phone beeped, his whole body jerked in shock. He grabbed his phone to silence it, and saw a text from Samantha.

Another car pulled up. It looks like Mitch. Hank can't be too far behind them.

Eddy stared at the message, then looked back into the building. There was still no way to see clearly who was inside, but he trusted Samantha's instincts. If she thought it was Mitch and Riley, then he was sure she was right. It shocked him that Hank would involve his child in his crimes. It was one thing to be crooked, but it seemed like he was intent on building a criminal empire.

There was no more time to waste. If Hank caught him there, he wasn't going to let him go. He started to turn back towards the parking lot, when he felt the sharp pressure of someone's grip on his shoulder. It was followed by the hard poke of a gun barrel against his side.

"Don't move."

Eddy held his breath. He knew with the slight tug of a finger his life would be over. He could see the reflection of his captor in the window before him. It was Riley. A brief relief flooded through him.

"Riley, just let me go, son. I won't make any trouble for you."

"Not a chance, Eddy. I knew when you were at the party that we should have silenced you, but Mitch said you were too old to be any threat. He's an idiot." He jerked him hard to the side. "Let's go. Don't make a sound." He yanked his cell phone out of his hand.

Eddy gulped as he wondered if he would realize that Samantha was in the car. He hoped not. As he was steered inside the building he didn't dare to look back over his shoulder.

"Mitch!" Riley shouted as he entered the business. "I got the other one!"

Eddy's heart sank as he realized what that meant. They already had Samantha. He was shoved into a small office, and there he saw Samantha tied up in a chair.

"Are you okay?" Eddy barely got the words out before he was slammed onto the floor by Riley.

"You couldn't stay away, huh? What did you think you were going to do here, old man?"

"Just let her go. She has nothing to do with any of this. Just let her walk, and I'll tell you both everything I know."

"We don't need to know anything you know." Riley chuckled. "Whatever you know is going to die with you tonight."

"Die?" Mitch's eyes widened. "Riley, we can't do that."

"Quiet, Mitch!" Riley snapped at him. "Just tie him up. Don't put them too close together, either."

Mitch pulled Eddy to his feet just long enough to push him down in a chair.

"Mitch, you don't have to do what he tells you. You can make your own decision here. So, you're dealing in some dirty money, that's no big deal, not compared to murder." He winced as Riley tied the ropes tight.

"Keep quiet." Mitch stood up and looked over at Riley. "What are we going to do now?"

"Just give me some time to think." Riley glared coldly in Eddy and Samantha's direction.

Samantha stared back at Mitch, her heart in her throat. Not long after she spotted Mitch, he had spotted her. She scrambled for the keys to start the car, but he came straight for her and dragged her out. She didn't even have time to scream before he had his hand over her mouth.

When Riley said he would kill them, Samantha believed him.

CHAPTER 17

"What are we going to do, Walt?" Jo jumped out of the car. Walt stepped out as well and caught her around the waist before she could bolt towards the building.

"Stop, Jo, just stop! We can't just rush in there. We don't know how many people could be inside, or how many weapons. We have to use good judgment here."

"Good judgment?" Jo gasped out the words. "I just saw Samantha get snatched up! We have to get her out of there!"

"You're right, we do." Walt narrowed his eyes. "But we can't do much to help her if we're dead, can we?"

"If only we had gotten here a few minutes earlier." Jo groaned.

"It wasn't my fault, there was construction." Walt frowned.

"I know that." She grabbed his shoulder with a gentle touch. "I'm not blaming you, Walt, really I'm not. I just can't stand here and wait, anything could be happening to her in there!"

"I know that, I do." He gritted his teeth. "And they likely have Eddy, too, otherwise we would have seen him by now. But if we move too fast, then they might both be killed. We need back-up."

"Let's call Brunner." Jo reached for her phone in the car.

"No, don't." Walt's tone was sharp. "We can't trust him, not with so much on the line."

"What do we do then?"

"I haven't seen Hank around at all."

"You think Hank isn't in on it?" She shook her head. "That's a big gamble."

"Yes, it is, but if he is in on it, it wouldn't make much of a difference would it. Mitch would tell him what's happening anyway and probably get him here to help out."

"True."

"I think it's a gamble we have to take. I don't

think we should call the cops. If we call in the cops, they'll bring in SWAT, or if they're involved in this they might try and set up Eddy and Samantha to take the fall. If SWAT comes in, who knows whether Eddy and Samantha will make it out alive." Walt grimaced. "I think Hank is our only chance besides going in there ourselves."

"But he's one of our main suspects, Walt, what if you're wrong?" Jo gazed at him with fear in her eyes. She didn't often feel it, but she was so worried about Samantha and Eddy.

"Just listen to me, Jo. I know what I'm doing." Walt dialed the number on his phone and pressed the phone to his ear.

"Walt, this seems like a really bad idea. Just hang up, please!"

Walt held up a finger to silence her.

"Hank?" He paused a moment. "No sorry, you don't know me. But I know you. I also know Mitch and Riley. I happen to know they are at Sunny River Property Investments right now. Did you know that?"

"What are you talking about?" Hank's tone sounded more flustered than angry.

"I think you need to get here." Walt hung up the phone.

"What did he say?" Jo stared into his eyes. "Did he know?"

"I don't know. I don't think so. But I guess we're going to find out for sure, soon." He looked back through the window of the building. "I think it's the best, possibly only, chance to save Eddy and Samantha."

"It seems like a big chance to take." She shook her head. "Maybe if we burst in, we could use the element of surprise and get them out."

"Maybe. Or we could force them to pull the trigger when they weren't even planning to in the first place. If Hank doesn't know what Mitch and Riley are up to then he might be able to stop them. At the very least it should buy us some time."

"Time that they might not have." She groaned. "What if he arrives and just tells them to take out the witnesses?"

"I don't know." Walt wrung his hands nervously. "I can't be certain of what will happen."

"I'm calling Brunner. Okay?"

"Yes, okay," Walt said. "I'm so worried about them, I don't think we have a choice."

"I agree." Jo dialed the number. It wasn't often that she reached out to law enforcement, after spending so many years behind bars, she preferred to avoid them. When his voicemail picked up, she knew she didn't want to leave her name behind, but she needed help for Eddy and Samantha. "Detective Brunner, this is Jo, Eddy's friend. Eddy and Samantha are being held inside of Sunny River Property Investments. We need back-up." She hung up the phone, then turned to Walt. "Do you think that was a mistake?"

"I don't know." He looked back towards the building as a large SUV pulled up to it. "But we're going to find out if my idea was a mistake first. Let's get closer." He led the way across the grass towards the building.

Jo listened closely, but she didn't hear any sirens in the distance. She wondered how long it would be before Detective Brunner would decide to check his voicemail. All she could do was hope that Walt had been right. She had good reason to believe in him. He usually was right.

~

*M*itch and Riley left Eddy and Samantha alone in the office, but the door remained open, and their harsh voices could be heard.

"Get out of here, I said." Mitch barked at someone. Samantha guessed that he was trying to minimize their exposure. He wanted as few people there as possible when he killed them. He was smart. She closed her eyes and tried to fight the fear that flooded through her.

"Eddy, I don't think that we're going to make it out of here." She strained her hands against the ropes around her wrists. "I've been trying to get this to loosen and it won't budge."

"You're supposed to be the positive one, Sam. Don't fail me now." Eddy stretched his fingers out towards her, but their chairs were too far apart to touch. "We're going to get out of this. We always do. We have good luck."

"Eddy, how? Even if we had a phone to contact the police, we couldn't trust that they would come to rescue us. They might be in on all of this."

"I can't tell you exactly how. But I know we're getting out of this. Just try to focus on what life is going to be like once we're out of here. I mean, Jo is going to owe both of us a lecture, don't you think? For taking so many risks."

"Yes, you're probably right." Samantha managed a small smile. "And Walt will have a whole list of things we did wrong." She was suddenly startled as the door to the company slammed open. Through the windows in the office, she saw Hank Greer stride in, his face red, and his eyes wild. He headed straight for Mitch and Riley, who seemed just as surprised to see him.

"What is going on here?" Hank gazed between them, then at Eddy and Samantha in the office. "What have you done?"

"Just calm down." Mitch patted his dad's shoulder. "We'll explain."

"I knew you would come and help," Riley said.

"Help with what?" Hank shrugged.

"The problem I have, of course." Riley shook his head.

"Problem?" Hank looked incredulous. "What are you doing? You need to let them go."

"No, we won't." Riley's eyes widened in realization as he drew his weapon. "We don't have to explain ourselves to him. We're in charge here, Mitch."

"Have you two lost your minds? Why do you have guns?" Hank's voice roared through the high ceilings of the building in the same moment that he drew his own weapon. "You'd both better start talking, I'm going to find out what's happened here one way or the other."

Eddy braced himself against the chair. He hoped he might be able to tip it over, but the wood was too solid. As he looked over at Samantha he could see the panic in her expression. Hank did seem startled by Mitch and Riley's actions, but that didn't mean they were safe.

"Dad, we're going to be rich!" Mitch stared at his father. "All we have to do is get through tonight and we'll have more money than we could ever count."

"You idiot." Hank took a step back. "How are you going to count money in jail?"

"I thought he would help us." Riley shook his head. "But now I know he's never going to be on our side, Mitch. He'd rather see us locked up than help us."

"You two have gotten yourselves into quite a mess." Hank sighed. He passed his gaze between them, then locked it on Riley. "Put your gun down."

"I won't."

"You will!" Hank demanded. "Look, you two have made a mess, and I'm going to do my best to help you clean it up. But I can't do that if you don't cooperate with me. Riley, put down the gun, and then we'll see about taking care of all of this."

"Taking care of?" Samantha mouthed to Eddy.

He nodded, his eyes narrowed, then looked back in the direction of Hank. He wasn't about to let the boys go down for the crime. Which meant the witnesses would have to be eliminated.

"Put it down, Riley." Mitch shook his head. "My dad's going to help us."

"Not likely." Riley frowned, but lowered his gun. "I thought he would, but now I don't think so."

Hank's phone beeped. "I better take this." He walked away as he put his phone to his ear.

The two boys spoke in voices so low that no one else could hear them.

Hank hung up then looked back at Mitch and Riley, his face red with fury. Then he turned away and called someone. He was speaking softly, but he seemed very agitated.

Samantha dug her nails into the rope that bound her wrists, but it was too thick to make any difference.

After Hank hung up he walked back over to Mitch and Riley as he tucked his phone back into his pocket.

"Just what did you think you were doing here?" Hank looked absolutely furious for a second, then he seemed to compose himself.

"We found out about this operation through

Orin, you know, we went to school with him. He managed to get us involved if we helped move some of the money through the furniture business. Don't act like you don't know anything about it. We saw you accepting cash from the owner of Sunny River." Riley crossed his arms.

"You saw that, did you?" Hank nodded. "Well, you're right. I do know about it." He stepped into the office where Eddy and Samantha were. "Untie them."

"Untie them? Why?" Mitch argued. "They're fine where they are for now. We need to work out a plan for what we are going to do with them."

"Untie them, now." Hank shot them both a look.

Mitch rushed over and began tugging at the rope around Samantha's wrists.

"Who did you call?" Riley stepped in front of Hank.

"Untie Eddy." Hank gave him a light shove. "Remember, how he helped you out years ago? This is how you return the favor?"

"I remember it very clearly. He wouldn't hesitate to turn us in tonight. They have both seen too much. We don't have any other options." Riley looked back at Mitch.

"Hey!" Samantha jumped up out of her chair.

"There's no need for that. We can keep our mouths shut. Can't we, Eddy?"

"Absolutely." Eddy strained against the ropes, his heart racing. He had no ability to protect Samantha while he was still tied up. "If you kill us, our friends will come forward with the information they know. They will ruin you. If you let us go, we'll all keep our mouths shut."

"Great, now their friends know, too." Mitch groaned. "I'm not going down for murder, Riley. I never agreed to that."

"No one is going to kill anyone." Hank rested his gun against the outside of his thigh and stared at the boys. "Both of you need to leave, now."

"What?" Riley blinked. "Just leave?"

"Why? What are you going to do?" Mitch frowned.

"I'm going to take care of the problem, that's what." Hank tipped his head towards the door. "Leave, now. I won't ask again."

Mitch and Riley exchanged troubled looks, then seemed to come to the same decision. As they bolted out through the door, Eddy could hear sirens in the distance. His chest tightened in anticipation of what would happen next. With the pressure of the police approaching, Hank could do anything, but most likely he would want to eliminate them. He rocked forward in his chair and tried to rip his hands free of the ropes. The sirens might not even be for them. How would they know? But that wouldn't matter to Hank.

Hank looked over at Eddy as the chair scraped against the floor.

"Stop, you're going to hurt yourself. Samantha, have a seat." Hank's head tipped towards the chair she'd recently been imprisoned in, then walked around behind Eddy. With a few tugs he was able to set Eddy's hands free. Eddy breathed a sigh of relief as the pain in his shoulders eased, but it was short lived, as Hank stood right behind him. "Both of you need to listen to me. We can't leave the building just yet. I need you to be patient."

"Just let us go, Hank, I know you want to protect your son, but the best way you can do that is by confessing everything that you've been involved in." Samantha slid to the edge of her chair and gazed up at him.

"There's nothing for me to confess." Hank looked hard into her eyes. "I am not your enemy here. Just be patient."

CHAPTER 18

*W*alt grabbed Jo's hand and pulled her back against the building as two men fled through the front door.

"I think that's Mitch and Riley."

"Where are they going?" Jo squinted through the darkness, then gasped as another figure approached the two men.

"Freeze!" The shout that carried through the nearly empty parking lot sent a shiver down her spine. She recognized the voice. It belonged to Detective Brunner. But why had he come alone? Where were the rest of the police?

Detective Brunner kept his gun trained on the two men.

"Get down on your knees."

"What are you going to do, Brunner?" Mitch demanded. "All you have to do is let us go, and we can make you richer than you could ever dream. Just put down your gun, we'll leave, and you'll be a wealthy man."

"Anything you want." Riley's voice shook. "We'll give it to you."

"You killed Colin for doing his job." Brunner kept his gun on them. "You killed him, because you wanted to be rich?"

"We didn't." Mitch kept his hands in the air. "I don't know who did that."

"No, I know you didn't, Mitch." Brunner shifted the gun slightly in Riley's direction. "Your friend did."

"Riley?" Mitch looked over at him. "Yeah right, he can't even throw a proper punch."

"You did it, didn't you, Riley? Colin came to you and tried to turn you against Mitch, didn't he?"

"Keep quiet." Riley groaned. "You can't prove any of that."

"Yes, I can." Brunner reached into his pocket with his free hand and a panicked voice began to play through the night air. It belonged to Riley.

"Hank, I'm in a big mess. I need your help, please. I've just killed Orin. He found out that I killed Colin and he was blackmailing me. He kept asking for more and more money. I don't know what to do. I killed them. I did it to protect Mitch, to protect both of us. I did it for all of us, but I'm worried I'm about to be caught. Please help me. Call me back."

"Riley, what did you do?" Mitch gasped out.

"This call was placed about an hour ago. But Hank never called you back, did he, Riley?"

"No. He didn't."

"He missed the message and it just came through about ten minutes ago. He saved the recording. He sent it to me. He wanted me to know what you had done."

"Why would he do that?" Riley shook his head. "I know, he wants all of the money for himself, that's why he never invited us into all of this. He was going to let us work ourselves to death, while he lived the good life."

"Riley Thomson, you're under arrest for murder." Detective Brunner pulled out his handcuffs.

Hank stepped out through the front door of the building and headed straight for Mitch and Riley. Behind him, Samantha and Eddy stepped out.

"Samantha! Eddy!" Jo bolted forward, startling

everyone as she jumped out of the shadows. "Are you both okay?"

"We're okay." Samantha wrapped her arms around her.

Walt nodded to both of them, his eyes wide with worry as he searched for any injuries they might have.

"The four of you." Brunner shook his head. "We have a lot to talk about."

Jo tried to hide behind Eddy as she realized that Hank would probably recognize her.

"Hank, how can you do this to us?" Riley squirmed against the handcuffs the detective placed on him. "Why didn't you just let us join you?"

"Boys." Hank shook his head as he gazed at them. "I was never a crooked cop. You should have known that. Everything I've made has been through legitimate investments. I've been working under-cover with a few other cops on this case for a long time. I was poised to take out everyone involved, soon. But it runs deep, lots of criminals involved and a couple of cops. I had no idea that you were part of it. We are working on taking down everyone involved. Unfortunately, now that includes the two of you. You took two people's lives, Riley. You murdered a good man, a stellar officer, and you are going to pay the price for that. You can't get away with that."

Eddy closed his eyes for a moment and savored those words. Colin and Orin would have their justice. A murderer was off the street, and it was a relief to know that Hank and most of the officers on the flash drive were on the right side of the law.

As Hank walked past Jo towards Detective Brunner, he glanced over at her. He took a few more steps then stopped and turned back to her.

"So." He shook his head and looked directly at Jo. "At least that explains why you broke into my place. You suspected me."

"You must be mistaken. I didn't break in." Jo stood straight and tried to hide the tremor in her voice.

"I don't think I am." He took a step closer to her. "I guess it was your lucky day that I didn't want to draw too much attention and risk blowing the case if you mentioned that money in the drawer."

"I guess so." She smiled.

"Just don't do it again."

She nodded and he turned away from her.

Jo breathed a sigh of relief as Hank walked away.

As several police cars pulled into the parking lot, Brunner led the four friends to a more well-lit area.

"You should know, Pete Havershed has been picked up. Thanks to your tip, Walt, about the pawn shop, we were able to trace him to a nearby motel. He's been arrested for possession of weapons. Apparently, he never planned on doing anything to Colin. But he did confess that he was going to use the weapons to threaten the person he is accused of assaulting originally. He claims that the victim had his stuff and money. The victim and him were meant to split it, but the victim was too greedy. Apparently, Peter originally assaulted the victim while trying to get his money and things back. It is a long-running feud. He also admitted to threatening the witness during the trial. He'll be going to prison now, that's for sure."

"Poor Colin, getting caught up in all of this." Samantha shook her head.

"Listen, I can understand why the four of you were hesitant to trust me after what you saw on that flash drive. But I hope you feel differently about things now. And Jo, I appreciate that you took a chance on me." Detective Brunner looked into her eyes. "I don't know what might have happened here tonight if you hadn't called Hank, Walt, or if you hadn't called me, Jo. But I know it wouldn't have been good. I honestly didn't even know that Hank and some other cops were involved in the investigation. I'm guessing Colin mustn't have either. I imagine that they've been undercover for so long in the operation. Eddy, I'm sorry for your loss." He held his hand out to him.

"Thank you, Detective." Eddy gave his hand a firm shake. "Good job."

"I try." He smiled some, then turned back to Hank and the boys, who were surrounded by other officers.

"I never expected Hank to turn out to be innocent in all of this." Jo stared at the man whose face was illuminated by the flashing lights. "I guess my instincts are getting pretty rusty."

"I wouldn't say that." Walt rested his hand on her shoulder. "You knew we could trust Brunner."

"I hoped." She cringed. "But it was a gamble."

"The important thing is that we have each other." Eddy glanced between all of them. "I mean that. If it weren't for the two of you, I don't think we would have made it out of there tonight."

"What happened to being positive?" Samantha gave him a light jab in the side.

"Okay, I'm positive we wouldn't have made it out of there. How's that?"

Samantha laughed as she tossed her arm around his shoulders.

"There have been studies that prove positive thought can have a strong impact on the circumstances of your life. Of course, there have also been studies that prove that positive thought is just a form of brainwashing."

"Take it easy, Walt." Jo gave him a light peck on the cheek. "You've done your duty for tonight."

"Thanks." He blushed as he gazed at her.

Samantha looked back over her shoulder as Mitch and Riley were led to a police car.

"You okay?" Eddy leaned close to her.

"It was a rough night." Samantha closed her eyes and rested her head on his shoulder.

"Yes, it was." Eddy slipped his arm around her waist. "Thanks for looking out for me, Sam."

"I always will, Eddy."

The End

ALSO BY CINDY BELL

SAGE GARDENS COZY MYSTERIES

Birthdays Can Be Deadly

Money Can Be Deadly

Trust Can Be Deadly

Ties Can Be Deadly

Rocks Can Be Deadly

Jewelry Can Be Deadly

Numbers Can Be Deadly

Memories Can Be Deadly

Paintings Can Be Deadly

Snow Can Be Deadly

Tea Can Be Deadly

CHOCOLATE CENTERED COZY MYSTERIES

The Sweet Smell of Murder

A Deadly Delicious Delivery

A Bitter Sweet Murder

DUNE HOUSE COZY MYSTERIES

Pups, Pilots and Peril

Tides, Trails and Trouble

DONUT TRUCK COZY MYSTERIES

Deadly Deals and Donuts

Fatal Festive Donuts

Bunny Donuts and a Body

BEKKI THE BEAUTICIAN COZY MYSTERIES

Hairspray and Homicide

A Dyed Blonde and a Dead Body

Mascara and Murder

Pageant and Poison

Conditioner and a Corpse

Mistletoe, Makeup and Murder

Hairpin, Hair Dryer and Homicide

Blush, a Bride and a Body

Shampoo and a Stiff

Cosmetics, a Cruise and a Killer

Lipstick, a Long Iron and Lifeless

Camping, Concealer and Criminals

Treated and Dyed

A Wrinkle-Free Murder

ABOUT THE AUTHOR

Cindy Bell is the author of the cozy mystery series Wagging Tail, Donut Truck, Dune House, Sage Gardens, Chocolate Centered, Macaron Patisserie, Nuts about Nuts, Bekki the Beautician, Heavenly Highland Inn and Wendy the Wedding Planner.

Cindy has always loved reading, but it is only recently that she has discovered her passion for writing romantic cozy mysteries. She loves walking along the beach thinking of the next adventure her characters can embark on.

You can sign up for her newsletter so you are notified of her latest releases at http://www.cindybellbooks.com.

Made in the USA
Lexington, KY
03 July 2019